FORGOTTEN
Promises

ELLE BROOKS

Copyright © 2014 Elle Brooks
This work is registered with and protected by Copyright House & UKCS.

Printed in the United States of America
First Edition: November 2014
Library of Congress Cataloging-in-Publication Data
  Brooks, Elle
    Forgotten Promises / Elle Brooks – 1st ed
    ISBN-13: 978-0-9929888-3-8

1.   Forgotten Promises—Fiction 2. Fiction—Romance
         3.   Fiction—Contemporary Romance

http://ellebrooksauthor.com

Blair and Ethan's story is fictitious, but the problems that they have to overcome are very real. If you have been affected by any of the issues raised in this book, there is always someone here to listen and help.

CANCER SUPPORT:

Macmillan Cancer Support –
http://www.macmillan.org.uk/Home.aspx

Leukemia and Lymphoma Society –
http://www.lls.org

DOMESTIC VIOLENCE AND ABUSE SUPPORT:

Childhelp National Child Abuse Hotline –
https://www.childhelp.org/hotline/

The National Domestic Violence Hotline –
http://www.thehotline.org

Prologue

Blair

Six Weeks Post Crash

I CAN HEAR soft piano music filtering through the muggy afternoon air as I cross the threshold, making my way down the cold stone aisle towards the altar. I can feel people staring, their gazes penetrating my skin as if each one physically presses upon me with the intensity of a searing hot branding iron. I'm all too conscious of the hushed whispers floating around in the desolate space. I'm shivering as I make my way to the front; I can't get a hold on my nerves. Voices that I don't recognize are uttering, "Is that the girlfriend? She was in the accident too, wasn't she?" They infiltrate my senses. Are these people really so ignorant that they have all forgotten this place is designed to carry noise? Each comment I catch as I near my destination feels more scathing than the last. I focus my attention on the vast grandeur of the stained-glass window at the front of the church and watch as the sun's midday rays pass through the colored panes, casting a rainbow that cascades down over the congregation of mourners. The bright hues are a stark disparity against the sea of black suits and white-collared shirts. There doesn't seem to be a single fleck of color on anyone's clothing, except the gold and red of the police decorations pinned proudly to the uniformed officers sporting them. Their brightness is a welcomed break in the monotonous army of glum clones.

My fingers are closed tightly around the stem of a single white rose. I didn't know if I should bring flowers or not, but now I wish I hadn't. I need to walk over to his coffin to lay it down; I hadn't thought of that. Bile rises in my throat, and the tears that have formed are threatening to fall. I'm holding my breath, eyes wide, willing them to dissipate as I return my focus once more to the window instead of the casket. It's too soon to be doing this again. The painful memory of Emily's funeral, still raw and exposed, sits unwelcomingly at the forefront of my mind. It's playing on an agonizing loop, taunting me, reminding me. The aesthetics couldn't be more different from hers, though; Emily's funeral service was akin to walking into a child's birthday party. Balloons adorned the ends of each pew in varying shades of shiny pink and purple latex. Cheerful, bright gerberas had been placed on every available surface, and there wasn't a single solitary piece of black clothing to be found. We had been given explicitly strict instructions to wear 'happy clothes' or she would 'haunt our asses for all eternity.' Em's words, not mine. There was to be no gloomy piano music, either; no nineties power-ballads of heartache and pain. Instead, the church was filled with dubiously dulcet tones from One Direction's *Story of My Life*. I'd practically scoffed when Em announced to me that she'd found the perfect funeral song. She proceeded to tell me that she'd narrowed it down to 1D or Bon Jovi's *Sleep When I'm Dead*. In any other circumstance, I'd have voted Bon Jovi all the way, but I had to concede on this one. I almost smile at the memory before realizing where I am and what I'm doing.

I slow my pace down, not wanting to reach my destination, but there's no avoiding it. In the next three steps I've reached the coffin. I can't prolong the inevitable any longer; I look down at the long mahogany box laid before me topped with what must be hundreds of roses. My whole body trembles as I reach out to place my flower amongst the other tributes. I catch my reflection against the highly polished surface of the wood and begin to feel dizzy. I blink attempting to refocus my vision as my fingers loosen their grip on the rose. My hand brushes against the cold hardwood and I pause briefly, wondering if it's time to wake up yet. Wishing for a different reality to the one I'm in at the moment. I hear Ethan's mom softly call out my name, but I can't move. I'm frozen in place by…I don't even know what, fear? Memories?

"Blair, honey…come sit by me." It's an order rather than request; suddenly she's by my side and ushering me to take a seat. I let her lead the way; it's just her sitting upfront.

"My mom couldn't find a parking spot; she'll be here any minute, is it okay for her to sit here too?"

"Of course, it is," she says and smiles weakly. "You're family."

I take in her appearance: her eyes are puffy and tired, and she looks completely worn out and defeated. Her cheeks look hollow, her hair is sitting limply on her shoulders and her lips are cracked and set into a thin line. She's a shadow of the woman Ethan first introduced me to months ago. The piano music stops and a minister approaches the lectern. I look wide-eyed at Moira and then glance at the empty seat where my mom should be right now, I need her here; I can't do this without her. I can't bear to sit through another funeral. Moira senses my anxiety and runs her hand down over my hair; she squeezes my shoulders and then pulls me into her side like my mom would do. The minister starts to speak, but I don't hear any words through the sound of the blood rushing in my ears. I can't do this. I'm not ready. I blink and let my first tear fall, no doubt carving the way for more to follow. I had agreed to come for Moira. I felt bad that she would have to face this alone. I look blankly towards the front but I can't see anything past my pain.

Chapter 1

Blair

BEFORE, WHENEVER I woke up from a dreamless sleep, I was disappointed that I couldn't remember anything; frustrated almost, that my imagination isn't impressive enough to muster up any subconscious nocturnal entertainment. These past three days I would give anything for that to still be the case. Every single time I close my eyes and try to contemplate a rest, I'm greeted with my own personal slideshow of horrifically vivid images. Ethan's unmoving body splayed at my feet, not breathing, the EMT's as they dragged me away.

The doctors have taken to sedating me, but in truth it makes everything feel worse. It blurs the lines of actuality, and for a fleeting moment I get to forget what has happened, what is still happening. It's cruel. When my mind starts to awaken from the medicated haze, I get to realize that the crash wasn't a nightmare all over again. I'm not at home tucked up in my warm cozy bed. I'm in a hospital in

1

Arizona recovering from surgery, and Ethan…hell, I can't even process a thought about him without crying. Each time it happens my mom presses the buzzer for the nurses to come and top up my meds.

I need to focus on accepting my new reality: Frank Jamison is paralyzed, the unsuspecting trucker that hit the rental car we were traveling in is dead, and Ethan may cease to exist. The thought is too painful, so this time it is me reaching for the buzzer.

Blair

Three Days Earlier. The Crash.

I OPEN MY eyes and everything looks to be in soft focus. I'm not wearing my glasses for some reason. Why am I not wearing my glasses? I lean forward, and a searing white-hot stabbing sensation spears through my body. I slump back into the position I was in, hoping it will bring some relief. I look down to see Ethan sprawled across me. Then it hits me. We crashed.

"Ethan?" My voice is hoarse and barely registers above a whisper. I'm overcome with a paralyzing fear as I stare down at the unnatural angle of his body. He's not moving.

"ETHAN!" I shout this time, ignoring the pain and protests from my body as I lean forward to try and rouse him. His chest isn't moving, and the terrifying recognition spikes my adrenaline. I look up to find the driver's seat empty. *Where's Frank?*

I don't know much about first aid and I'm sure that you're not supposed to move someone that's been involved in a crash, but Ethan's not breathing and I can't attempt CPR in the position we are both in.

I've seen in the news mothers that have single-handedly lifted a car that has trapped their child, their bodies overcome with an adrenaline rush so powerful they become almost superhuman. I think I must be experiencing something akin to that right now, because Ethan is 6.3" and around 180 pounds, yet I pull him from the car like he's a toddler. I look around and see that the driver of the truck we collided with has blood gushing from his head and he's swaying back and forth, frantically shouting into his cell.

I look back at Ethan and start to panic as I struggle to remember what I know about CPR. I blow two breaths into his mouth and then begin compressions on his chest while my tears blur my already compromised vision. I'm not sure how long I do this, but I'm acutely aware of sirens in the distance, and I'm praying to a god that I've never really been sure I believe in that they hurry up and reach us.

My arms are aching, and I'm out of breath as an EMT pulls me away from Ethan. I'm frantically kicking and screaming for them to let me stay with him as one of them ushers me into the back of an ambulance, while the other hovers over Ethan. I can hear people talking over the little radio attached to the guys' uniform; they're requesting more assistance. I hear the word body bag being spoken before the gravity of the situation hits me with the force of a thousand bullets and my world finally goes black.

ele

I slowly wake as I'm being lifted from a gurney into a hospital bed. The doctors are firing questions at me. What's my name? Can I tell them the date? What happened? My mind is foggy, and all I can focus on is that I can't see Ethan anywhere.

"Please, where's my boyfriend? Is he okay?"

"I'm not sure yet, miss. Just please lie back while we check you over," a doctor replies as I attempt to sit up, and he gently takes hold of my shoulders and presses me back down onto the bed.

"No stop, please I need to find Ethan." I move to climb down and again he pushes me back. "He wasn't breathing; I need to know he's okay. Let me go!" My words are distorted by my desperate sobs, and more people have gathered around me and are now trying to hold me in place. I feel a sharp jab in my leg and watch as the nurse struggles to give me a shot while I'm flailing my arms and legs around trying to slip from her grasp. My body starts to feel heavy as I struggle. Everything begins to move in slow motion and blur until I can't keep my eyes open any longer and begin to lose consciousness.

I feel as though all I did was blink, but the darkened room I'm in tells me that's not the case. I move and shuffle around on the bed, trying to relieve the discomfort I'm feeling around my stomach and realize I'm hooked up to IV's. I have cannulas in one of my arms that look to be leading back to a small blue machine. The steady beep, beep, beep is the only sound breaking the otherwise silent

4

ambiance. I reach down and realize I have a dressing over my stomach. It hurts to move, but I need to find out what's happening. I press the call button beside me and a nurse appears in the doorway almost instantly. After she explains that I'd been suffering from a ruptured spleen, which subsequently has just been removed, the nurse leaves to go and get a doctor to authorize more pain relief.

My mom walks slowly through the door with a coffee in hand, looking exhausted. She glances at me in the bed and then halts momentarily. I wait as the recognition sets in that I'm awake, and she rushes towards me, placing the cup on the stand beside the bed.

"Sweetheart, how are you? Gosh, you had me scared, baby girl." Her words are spoken in a loud exhale, like the weight of the world has just been lifted from her shoulders. She looks beyond tired, and her eyes are glassy and rimmed red. I can tell she's trying to hold back tears. I'm hoping like hell that they are tears of relief and not anything more sinister.

"How are you here? I don't understand," I say, squeezing my eyes closed as I shake my head in confusion. My voice feels all scratchy, and I ache from the top of my head to the tips of my toes.

"I was already on my way to come collect you. Frank called me and told me about you and Ethan being arrested. I was only an hour away when I got a phone call from the hospital letting me know you'd been brought here. Goodness Blair, I thought I was going to lose you."

She squeezes my hand lightly and finally loses the battle to keep her tears at bay.

"What's happened to Ethan, Mom? Have you heard

anything? No one is letting me know if he's okay. You have to go find out," I plead and then pause as I notice a somber expression move across her face.

"Oh god no, please tell me he's okay. He has to be okay!"

"Shh, calm down Blair," she says in a hushed tone, wiping the tears that are now racing down my face with her thumbs.

"He's in the ICU; he's in a coma and that's all that I know, honey. Frank is in the ICU, too." I stiffen at the mention of him.

"This, this is his fault," I stammer trying to calm my breathing. "He just stopped in the middle of the road to pick a fight with Ethan. Who does that?" Her eyebrows pull together as she's about to reply to my accusation, when the nurse returns with more pain relief. A milky white liquid is being injected into the drip at the side of the bed; within a few seconds I feel the aches start to lessen in their intensity. It makes my body feel strange, like somehow it's not my own, and I'm witnessing everything that's happening from somewhere else. Mom goes out into the hall to speak with one of the doctors, leaving me with the knowledge that my boyfriend is in a coma. I'm not sure if I should be terrified of that, or thankful. I know it's bad to be in a coma, but for a moment I thought she was going to tell me that he was dead. I've experienced my fair share of loss already; I don't think I could bear anymore. If Ethan dies it will break me. I've already lost two people I love.

It dawns on me that Mom said that Frank was in the ICU too. I've never been someone that wishes bad things on other people, but I'm struggling at the moment because although I know it's terrible to admit, I hope that asshole dies.

Chapter 2

Ethan

I WANT TO open my eyes but it's not happening, and I don't understand what's wrong. I can hear voices and beeping. Why won't my eyes open?

"There's been no change, I'm afraid. We are monitoring him very closely, Mrs. Jamison. You should go and get something to eat; you've not left the room all day."

"I know and I will, I just don't like leaving him on his own."

Mom? That's her voice—I'm sure of it; it's so faint, but it's definitely hers. I want to turn towards it, but I can't. God, what the hell is wrong with me? Why can't I move? Shit, my head hurts. I'm so tired, but I'm in too much pain to sleep and I can't lift my eyelids. Maybe I'm dreaming. Can you feel pain in a dream? I'm confused and this headache feels real.

The beeping is getting louder. I need it to stop. Concentrate, Ethan—open your fucking eyes, goddamn it.

Beep.

Beep.

Beep,

Beep, beep, beep, beep, beep.

"Doctor, someone please come quick! Something's happening!"

"Mom?" *Wait did I say that aloud?* I try again, but all I can muster up is a cough. My throat hurts. There's something in my mouth and it's making me gag; I need it out.

"Oh, thank you, god! Thank you. Ethan honey, I'm here!"

My eyes start to flutter as I concentrate on trying to open them. I finally manage and then instantly wish I hadn't. I'm greeted with ridiculously bright fluorescents and my headache takes on a whole new dimension. There's so much pressure building behind my eyes I almost want someone to drill a hole into my temple to drain it. Mom's face moves into view, shielding the brightness for a moment before it's replaced with a woman's face that I don't recognize. She's leaning over me and telling me to keep calm while she removes the ETT. What the fuck's an ETT?

She starts pulling at something and then I gag as a long tube scrapes its way up my throat and out of my mouth. It steals my breath and leaves me feeling like she's just sandblasted my esophagus. The machine next to my head is going nuts, shrieking and beeping. The woman disappears from vision moments before the room falls quiet. I sigh in relief and attempt to sit up. My surroundings look completely sterile with a saccharine greenish blue tinge to it. Or maybe it has no color at all and it's my blurred spotted vision that's painting the room.

"Whoa, hold your horses, mister. Please lie back down. The doctor is on his way to see you."

Doctor? What the hell is going on?

"Ethan honey," Mom says softly as she leans over me and brushes my hair from my forehead.

"What's going on?" I manage to ask. My throat is on fire, and nothing is making any sense to me.

"You were in an accident, honey. Do you not remember?"

I register her words, but it's like someone has thrown a thick woolen blanket over my thoughts. I don't know what she's talking about.

"Ah, nice to see he's awake." A male voice booms through the room and I wince at the volume.

"My name is Doctor Moss, Ethan. How are you feeling?" I look over to see a short fat guy in a white coat that barely covers his plaid shirt and bright red bow tie. His curly red hair is combed to the side and he's studying a chart before his eyes lift from behind the rim of his round golden spectacles to meet mine. He looks like a poster child for a nutty professor.

"Everything hurts," I tell him. He smiles and reassures me that he can give me something to make me more comfortable. I don't know what it is that he's planning to give me, but I hope to fuck he gives me a truckload of it, and fast.

"Ethan can you tell me your full name, please?"

I look at him confused. I can see from here that the clipboard he's holding has Ethan Jamison scrawled over it. Why the hell's he asking?

"Ethan Jamison," I reply.

"Excellent. Can you tell me what month and year we are in?"

What the hell? If he doesn't know what year we are in he really has no business working in a hospital; he should be a patient.

"It's February 2014. What's with the questions?" I say as I bring my hand up to rub at my throat. I'm attached to wires and tubes and god only knows what else. They bite at my wrist where they disappear under a bandage. I move my attention back up to the doctor and catch the look he and my mom are sharing.

"Ethan, it's not Feb—" Mom's silenced by doctor what's-his-face raising his hand. She rears her head back a little and looks concerned.

"I'm afraid that's not quite correct; it's June 2014," he says eying me carefully.

"Oh…I, wait, I'm confused. June?"

"Yes, Ethan, June 2nd. Do you remember anything from the accident you were involved in?"

I'm officially starting to worry; nothing is making sense. It can't be June and I have no idea what accident he's talking about. I look over to my mom, who is looking about as confused as I feel, and then back at my wrist that's aching like a bitch. I scan the room, although I have no clue what I'm looking for, and then try and shake the cloud that seems to have settled over my mind. I feel like I'm being suffocated in the swath of pale green cotton blankets that have me bound to the bed. "Sorry, I don't know. I can't think straight."

"Not to worry, Ethan, the nurse will be right through with some medication for the pain. Just try and relax, and I'll be back soon," he says, placing the chart he was holding on the bottom of the bed.

"I'll be right back, honey," Mom calls as she hurries to follow the doctor out of the room.

Just relax—is that a fucking joke? How the hell does he expect me to relax? There isn't a part of me that's not hurting right now. I have no idea how or why I've woken up in here, and apparently I've just lost four months of my life somewhere. Relaxed is the last thing I'm feeling.

Chapter 3

Blair

I'M GOING CRAZY being cooped up in this drab, depressing room. I shouldn't complain; it could be worse, I guess. I could be out on the ward with only a flimsy lavender-colored curtain to provide any semblance of privacy. Having my own room must be costing my mom a fortune. She's currently asleep in the chair by the side of my bed, and she looks so peaceful I don't want to wake her. I'm pretty sure she hasn't slept at all since I was brought in here two days ago. The doctors have apparently approved me to be released either tomorrow or the next day, providing that my stats are all good and the stitches from my surgery are healing as they should. They're mistaken if they think I'm going anywhere without seeing Ethan. I've begged and pleaded for them to let me go and visit with him. I'm not family though, so they won't let me into the ICU. The nurse stationed at the end of the hall has escorted me back here twice already. I figured I could sneak out and go find him. I'm not as stealthy as I hoped I'd be, hooked up to this stupid IV. The wheels on the drip stand sound like a freaking freight train against the tiled floor. She told me that there was no use trying to creep into the high dependency unit, as you have to buzz through to gain access. Stupid hospital.

The afternoon sunlight is filtering through into my room; I've spent the last hour watching dust molecules float daintily through the streams the blinds make and then disappear as they move into the shade. I'm envious of them; I wish I could just vanish. Slip into the shadows like the dust, hiding in plain sight. That way I could go and find Ethan.

elle

I can't take lying in here anymore. I cover Mom with one of the mint-colored cellular blankets from the bed and creep out of the room as quietly as I can without waking her, gingerly making my way down the hall towards Nurse Battleax. That's not her actual name, although I think it should be. She's not the vision you have in your head of a typical caregiver. In fact, she's what your mind would conjure up at the phrase, 'heavy metal groupie': her hair is streaked with blues and greens—from her roots I'd guess she's blonde—and piled messily on top of her head, showing off the tattoos that adorn the skin on the back of her neck. All I've been able to make out so far are a few swirls and a couple of tiny stars that disappear under her collar; it looks as though someone went to town on her with a pack of bright-colored Sharpies. I'm pretty intrigued as to what the full tattoo looks like. Her ears are pierced with those spacer earrings; I could probably push my pinky through the void in her lobe if I tried, although I guess she wouldn't take kindly to it. Her whole appearance screams 'stay away'. She has kind eyes, though; if you focus on those and not the permanent scowl her mouth seems to be set into.

"Miss Thomas, I don't want to have to escort you back to your room again. Please accept that you are not allowed into the ICU," she says in a bored tone as I approach the desk.

"Relax, I just want to go find the cafeteria. I'm bored and I need to stretch my legs." She studies me for a few beats, no doubt trying to discern whether or not it's a ploy to go on some twisted scavenger hunt for my boyfriend.

She narrows her eyes at me before dropping her shoulders a little. "Fine, but please don't make me regret this," she says standing and stretching to hold the door open for me.

I duck under her arm, but the top of my drip stand catches her and she glares at me like I've just tried to hurt her on purpose. "Sorry," I utter, feeling the need to apologize, even though she's the one that positioned herself so precariously. I make my way down the long barren corridor before coming to the bank of elevators. I study the enormous blue sign above the call buttons until I see that there's a coffee shop on the ground floor. I'm wearing my spare glasses that I keep loose in my purse; my regular ones were lost in the accident. I busy myself rubbing the lenses with the hem of my shirt as I rock back and forth on my toes waiting for the elevator to descend. The glass is covered in tiny scratches where it's scuffed against my keys and heaven knows what else lurking in the depths of my bag. The doors finally open, and I'm rapidly assaulted by the smell of freshly ground coffee. I inhale as much as my lungs can take and hold the bitter, rich aroma for a few seconds before breathing it out slowly. I hate the smell of hospitals; I have since the day Em was diagnosed. The coffee scent is masking the clinical bleach smell that the rest of the building holds, and I find myself wondering if they'll let me sleep down here tonight. I join the back of the line and wait to place my order as some guy wearing sunglasses trips over the base of my drip stand. It teeters a little before he manages to grab hold of it and stop it toppling over completely.

"Sorry. I'm sorry," he rushes to apologize as I look up and realize everyone in the line is staring.

"Blair!" Moira, Ethan's mom, shouts from the front where she's being served and ushers people out of the way as she makes her way back through the ten or so people in front of me.

"No worries, I'm fine," I say, shooing the guy away and turning my attention back to my boyfriend's mom.

"Moira, how…how's Ethan?" I stammer as my mouth suddenly feels like it's been stuffed to capacity with cotton balls. I have an overwhelmingly unexpected urge to cry, and my throat constricts as I wait for her reply.

"Madam! Madam, excuse me. You've forgotten your drink," the barista shouts and Moira holds her finger up to me, and then rushes back to the front of the line to collect her coffee. She's back moments later and guides me to a window seat and sits down.

"He woke up a few hours ago," she says with a small smile on her face that doesn't look quite right; it's a sad smile.

My stomach knots as I wait for her to continue. I can hear the blood rushing about in my ears, and I feel a chill run down my spine in anticipation of her next sentence. She looks down at her coffee before meeting my gaze and then lets out a small sigh. Shit, that can't be a good sign. The coffee shop is painted a deep red and fitted out with rich eggplant and cherry-colored fabric seating and oak bistro tables. It has a warm and cozy atmosphere; or at least it did, until Moira's expression gives me chills. I shiver involuntary and fold my arms across my chest in dreaded anticipation.

"He's still very confused, and he doesn't remember anything about the accident. He's drifting in and out of consciousness, but the doctors have assured me that it's a normal response," she says softly.

I let out the breath I was holding and allow my shoulders to drop. "Thank god he's awake," I tell her, moving my glasses to rub my eyes in an effort to try and disperse the tears that are gathering in tiny pools. "I'm so relieved; the doctors wouldn't tell me anything about his condition and refused to let me come see him because I'm not family."

"You poor thing. I'm so sorry I didn't come to find you and update you. It just didn't cross my mind." She reaches across the table and rubs my arm calmly in apology. I attempt to smile but it's strained and weak as she places her hand over mine.

"He's bruised and sore; he'd dislocated his shoulder,

sprained one of his wrists, and he must have hit his head pretty hard in the accident. He had swelling around his brain, and they had to do a procedure to alleviate some of the pressure." My eyes widen in horror as she squeezes my hand slightly. "No, no, he's okay now—he's stable. He's just a little dazed and confused. Hopefully, he'll be feeling a little better when he wakes up. He's been given some pretty heavy-duty pain medication that's got him slipping in and out of sleep."

"I need to see him," I tell her through a sob as I reach forward and steal the napkin from under her drink to wipe my eyes.

"Come with me, sweetheart," she says, standing up and letting her chair scrape against the floor. A young couple swoops in like vultures, takeaway cups and pastries in hand, waiting to descend on the table in the busy shop. "Let's see what we can do."

Chapter 4

Ethan

"LOOK WHO'S HERE to see you, Ethan."

I lazily turn toward the door as Mom's voice cuts through the antiseptic atmosphere of this hospital room. I hate it. The hum of the machines, the constant beeping of the monitors, the smell of alcohol wipes—the combination is making my head swim. I'd do anything for some fresh air to try and clear the fog I'm in.

Mom steps to the side as she enters the room and a captivating sight fills the doorway. I smile and take in the vision in front of me. Before I can manage to string a set of coherent thoughts together, she's made her way over to the bed and thrown her arms around me in a firm yet gentle hug. Not that I'm not enjoying having her pressed against me or anything, but my eyes widen as I look at my mom. I'm not really a touchy-feely person, especially with people I don't know.

Mom notes the confusion that must be pretty evident

on my face, and the girl tenses and then leans back, look-ing at me. Her expression appears almost hurt, like she was expecting a hug back or something. This is awkward.

"Blair's been so worried about you. She hasn't been allowed in until now. I struck a deal with the nurse; she can only be in here a couple of minutes," Mom says, watching for my reaction a little too closely.

"Oh." I'm not sure what they're expecting me to say; I have no idea why she'd want to be in here.

Blair moves slowly back from the bed and glances at my mom and then back to me, looking as confused as I feel.

"Ethan, you know who I am, right?" she asks scrunching her nose and causing her black hipster looking glasses to slip a little.

I shift slightly and shake my head. "Sorry, no. I have no idea, I've seen so many nurses come and go out of here today already."

This is obviously not what she wanted to hear; her eyes glaze over, and she whirls around to look at my mom who's staring at me like I've just grown another head.

"Sweetheart, this is Blair, your girlfriend."

Girlfriend? I look back to Blair, who's now wiping furiously at her eyes. Shit, she's crying. I don't do girl-friends, never have—I've always favored hook-ups; that way I can be in, out and on my way without any drama. I pinch the bridge of my nose and then chance another quick glance at her. I wish I hadn't; my chest feels like it's being squeezed as I take in how broken she looks.

"I, I don't understand," I manage but this just seems to fuel the poor girl's upset emotional state even more.

"I'm just going to fetch a doctor," Mom announces, leaving me here with Blair. I have no idea what to say to her. How can she be my girlfriend? I've never seen her before. I feel bad that I'm making her cry.

"I'm sorry," I offer quietly. I don't know why I'm apologizing, but it seems like the right thing to do. She gives me a sad smile, but it only makes me feel worse. She seems almost embarrassed as she lowers her gaze to the floor. I'm uncomfortable as hell with this whole situation, but I can't take my eyes off of her. I want to make her feel better, but I have no idea how. She's fiddling with the hem of her long sleeved grey t-shirt. I watch in fascination as she picks invisible lint from her shirt, then from her yoga pants. Her head is down but she keeps glancing in my direction, then diverting her eyes when they meet mine.

Mom marches into the room with Doctor Moss hot on her heels. She asks Blair to step outside with them and then all three leave the room. I can just about see their heads from the internal window that faces into the hall. They've gathered outside for privacy, no doubt while they talk about me. No one closed the door as they left, though, and I can hear every word they're saying. They should have just stayed in the room. Now I feel like a dick eavesdropping, but they're speaking about me so I'm straining to make sure that I can hear everything.

"You said everything had gone well with the operation and that he might be a little confused; that's not confused! He had no idea who Blair was," my mom says hurriedly.

"Mrs. Jamison, with all due respect brain injuries are very complicated. We often can't perceive the extent of the damage until the patient comes around. It's perfectly normal in cases like Ethan's for the patient to be confused, or experience some short-term memory loss."

I'm trying to process what that all means when I hear Blair's voice interject.

"He had no idea at all who I was. How can he not re-member me, yet he knows who Moira is?"

"Like I've said, head injuries are very unpredictable. There are different areas of the brain that house short and long-term memory. It's likely that the swelling Ethan ex-perienced from the accident has resulted in his memory lapse."

"Will this be permanent?" I hear Mom ask in an anx-ious voice.

"It's too early to determine that, Mrs. Jamison. We'll be running more tests over the next few days. It may be the case that his memory will return to normal in its own time."

Fuck. I rub at my eyes with the heel of my hand and try relaxing my shoulders. How can this be happening to me?

elle

Blair didn't return to my room after the discussion out in the hall. I was kind of relieved at first, but now a little time has passed and I have an overwhelming urge to speak with her. How can I have forgotten my own girlfriend? I have so many questions that I want to ask her. How long have we been in a relationship? Where did we meet? Are we serious? I suppose I could ask my mom, but that just wouldn't feel right. I need for them to tell me about the accident; I still don't know what happened other than that it was a car crash. I've been back from my CT scan about fifteen minutes when my mom returns to my room.

"How are you feeling, honey? Did the doctors say anything more to you?"

"It was fine," I answer. "I have to wait for Doctor Moss to come and explain the results."

She takes the light blue leatherette seat by the side of the bed and rubs small circles into her temples.

"So, I've been talking to the doctors."

"Okay, well by the sound of your voice, I'm guessing they didn't tell you what you wanted to hear?" She smiles, but it doesn't reach her eyes, and it confirms my suspicion. "Let me guess: they've realized my brain's wired wrong?"

"No...they couldn't find it!" she deadpans; it lightens the atmosphere for a nanosecond before the black cloud that seems to be following me descends on the room once more.

"Seriously though, Ethan, what can you remember? Did you not recognize Blair at all?"

"The last thing I can remember is practicing for the entrance exam for Eastman," I tell her. "I don't remember anything about Blair; I don't even recognize her from school. Does she even go to West Point?"

"Yes," is her only reply. We sit in an uncomfortable silence for what feels like an eternity.

"The doctors have advised me not to tell you any information about the crash; they think stress will hinder your memory returning. They want to wait and see if it starts to come back on its own." I look at her and wonder if she's joking for a moment, but her eyes are telling me that she's not.

"This is bullshit!" I'm not sure why I'm raising my voice at her, but I'm beyond frustrated. "I have no fucking clue what I'm doing here. I've lost months of my life, and I'm not even allowed to ask why? Way to go on not stressing me out." I know my heart rate has increased by the little machine displaying it at the side of the bed. I have an overpowering desire to smash the hell out of it. I feel so helpless. I hear my dad's voice ring through my mind, telling me I'm pathetic and it stops my sudden rage-fuelled outburst dead in its tracks.

"Where's Dad?"

Mom's face falls; it doesn't bode well and I'm positive it can't be a good sign.

"I um…I'm not sure if the doctors would want me to tell you," she says sheepishly.

"What the fuck Mom, just tell me where he is!" I shout, and she cowers back in her seat. I immediately feel like a prick. I'm acting like my father and I hate it.

"He's in the hospital, too," she finally concedes. "He was in the accident with you and Blair."

Wait, what? Was Blair in the accident, too? "I don't understand. Dad, Blair and I were all in the accident?" I ask.

"Yes, you were all in the car, your dad had come to collect you."

I'm desperately trying to access some small memory, anything to tell me why we would all be in a car together. I hate the asshole; he's the last person on earth I'd call to come and collect me from anywhere.

"Why hasn't he been in here?" I ask. She runs her fingers over her hair, then leans forward resting her forehead in one hand. "He's in the ICU too; he can't come in here."

I'm about to ask what's wrong with him, but I stop myself when I realize that I don't even care. "Oh," is all I manage. It's probably not normal for a son not to want to know if his dad is okay, but then again, it's probably not normal for a father to beat his son whenever the mood strikes. I let out a long breath in comprehension of the fact that if I were told that he was dead right now I'd be relieved.

I squeeze my eyes shut and wish I could just remember Blair, even if it were just one tiny little thing, any minute detail; I'd take it. Her tear-stained face has been haunting me since she left the room this afternoon. I can't shake the image from my mind, and it's like her pain was tangible, a completely solid entity that I could have reached out and grasped. It dawns on me that she had an IV stand with her when she was in here earlier; I have an unexpected need to know if she's okay. I'm not sure why, but her hug felt like the only thing that has made sense to me since I woke up in this nightmare. Considering the clusterfuck of a situation I'm lying in right now, I could really use another one.

Chapter 5

Blair

IT'S A DREAM; it has to be. No, not a dream, a night-mare. One of those horribly vivid Technicolor ones that you need to lie still and spend ten minutes untangling to determine whether it really happened. The kind of night-mare that leaves you breathless, trembling in a cold slick sweat. Yes, that's it. I'm having a nightmare; I just need to try relaxing, and it'll be over soon. I'll wake up. I'm clutching onto that notion until the nurse removes the can-nula from my arm, the sharp scrape of the needle being removed against my sensitive, sore skin lets me know that I'm very much awake. I watch in morbid fascination as the tiny puncture wound starts to seep deep crimson droplets of blood; I can smell the metallic tang.

"Here, hold this cotton bud to your arm tightly. It will stop soon," the nurse says passing me a small fluffy white bud that looks like cotton candy. I take it from her and press it to my arm as instructed. I don't trust my voice not to crack, so I don't attempt any form of response. Instead, I remain silent and focus on breathing in and out, in and out, inhale, exhale. *You're fine, Blair,* I tell myself. My emotions are winning out; I feel anything but fine. My vision is starting to blur from the tears that are gathering in the corners of my eyes.

"Are you okay, sugar?" the elderly plump nurse asks. "You should have let me know if you have a phobia about needles."

I smile and nod my head. She eyes me carefully for a few seconds. "Okay then, that's the IV all out. Just press the buzzer if you need anything," she says, already halfway out of the room.

Mom went back to her hotel to shower and change into a clean set of clothes. I was thankful to be left on my own, but now I wish I wasn't. He didn't know me. There wasn't a single spark of recognition in his beautiful azure eyes. I replay the whole sorry interaction like a movie stuck on a loop in my mind. The first tear falls and bursts the damn, more are quick to follow. The silent tears turn to sobs, the sobs turn to wails and then before I know it I'm pounding my fists as hard as I can into the bed in complete and utter frustration. By the time I've calmed down, my arms are aching, and I have the beginning of a headache forming behind my eyes. The throbbing around my stitches is a welcomed distraction from the emotional pain. This is so unfair! Why is this happening? I should be happy that Ethan woke up, but I can't focus on anything other than the agony I feel coursing through my heart. He doesn't even know who I am.

elle

"Blair?" Moira whispers as she takes a seat next to my bed. "Honey, are you awake?"

I don't think I can do this; I don't want to talk to anyone, I just want to lie here and pretend that none of this is happening. I'm contemplating keeping my eyes closed and faking sleep. Maybe if I don't respond she'll leave again.

"Blair, Ethan's asking for you."

This has my attention. I bolt upright in bed, pushing the covers away from me and ignoring the smarting in my stomach that the erratic movement caused. "He's asking for me?"

She gives me a small smile and nods her head gently. "Yes."

"Wait, does that mean he remembers me?" My voice has risen a few octaves with the hope that's surging through me. Her face falls and she looks like she's about to cry.

"No honey, not yet."

I feel my body sag as I release a long breath. "Oh."

I excuse myself to the bathroom and splash water on my face; I'm hoping that it will quell the heat in my cheeks and dampen the overbearing desire I have to cry again. I look at the reflection staring back at me and almost don't recognize it. My eyes are puffy and red behind my glasses, my face is blotchy from the huge volume of tears that have rained over my cheeks, and my hair is limp and lifeless. I feel like I should care, but in truth I don't. I have zero energy and feel completely drained. I look down at my watch and realize that my mom's been gone almost two and a half hours; she should be back soon.

I follow Moira down the hall to the elevators, and as we step in I notice she doesn't press the button for the ICU. I rock back and forth on my toes as she glances over and catches my confusion. She tells me that Ethan was being transferred to a different ward before she came to my room. The elevator descends and then comes to a stop at floor eleven. "This is us," she says as I follow her lead and stop by the ward's entrance so we can sanitize our hands. There's no buzzer for the door; I guess anyone can visit, unlike the protocol upstairs. We make our way through the doors and down the dingy mint green corridors until we reach the room at the very end. Ethan's sitting on the bed with his cell in his hands, swiping the screen and eyeing it like it's some foreign contraption.

"Blair's here honey," Moira announces as I walk in behind her and stand at the bottom of the bed feeling completely self-conscious. A couple of days ago I would have walked into the room, and thought nothing of taking a seat in Ethan's lap. Now I feel like an intruder, like I'm an unwelcome guest.

I hate it.

He throws the phone onto the bedside table and looks up at me with a small smile. My heart feels like it stutters in my chest as his dimples flash, and I want so desperately to run over and kiss him, to climb into his lap and cling to him. I want to tell him that I've never been so scared as I have been over these past few days, not knowing if he was okay. His wrist is bandaged, he has a small dressing on the side of his head, and the hair around it looks to have been shaved. There's a yellowing bruise on his cheekbone and he's sporting more scruff on his face than I've ever seen on him before, yet he's still beautiful. I settle for a small wave and then drop my hand quickly. Who waves, honestly? God, I hate how awkward this feels. The room is filled with an uneasy silence, and Moira informs us that she's leaving me to visit with Ethan while she goes and grabs another coffee. I don't know if I'm relieved that she's going or if I'm scared to be here by myself. Moira had mentioned that the doctors have asked that we let him try and recover his memories on his own, not push him or cause any unnecessary stress that could prolong his condition. I have absolutely no idea what I'm allowed to say to him.

"So," he says nodding his head and I just stare blankly back at him.

"We're dating?" I'm not sure if it's a statement or a question so I just nod my head in agreement.

"Come sit down—you're making me nervous," he huffs while throwing me a dazzling white smile and patting a spot on the bed next to him. I almost leap at the chance to be closer to him, but I calm myself and move around the bed slowly and sit facing him, Indian-style.

"I've got to admit, this feels pretty surreal and a little awkward," he says looking straight into my eyes.

"Ha, it really does," I say with a small smile. "It's worse than that first day in the library." He gives me a strange look and then I realize that he has no idea what I'm talking about. He can't remember staring at my boobs in the library the first time we ever spoke because he can't remember me. I shake my head in a gesture that's meant to say, *never mind.*

"I—"

"We—"

We both start to talk at the same time and then freeze.

"You first," we say in unison and then laugh.

"Jinx," he says and winks. It's playful and familiar, and I want to burst into tears all over again that I can't lean forward and just kiss him. He's staring at me so intently that I don't quite know what to do with myself. I fiddle with the hospital band around my wrist and wait for him to fill the silence.

"You're beautiful," he tells me. "How did I manage to con you into dating me?"

My shoulders relax a little, and I let the warmth of his complement wash over me. I sigh inwardly and revel in the first soothing and cheerful feelings I've had since he woke up not knowing me.

"I think you drugged me," I reply. He laughs, and it makes my heart soar.

"So I guess that we're pretty serious?" His face is lowered, and he looks up at me through his long dark eyelashes. Men shouldn't be allowed to have lashes that perfect.

"My screen saver is of you, sleeping." He smiles almost bashfully as he looks over at his phone.

"You have a picture of me sleeping?" I reply, surprised, and his cheeks color immediately. He stutters and tries to respond, but it's obvious he has no clue what to say.

"Relax, it's fine, I just didn't realize you had a picture of me asleep. If you go through your photo stream there'll be plenty of pictures of us goofing around." I'm not sure why I just told him to do that. How awful must it be to see pictures of a time and a person that you can't recollect? Nice going, Blair.

"I've already gone through them," he answers with a hint of a cocky grin playing at his lips. "Look, I know this is weird but when I saw you earlier, even though I didn't remember you, seeing you cry hurt."

I look up at him a little startled by his admission and wait for him to continue. I can feel my heart slamming against my chest, and it's taking all my energy to stop myself from crawling over the bed and taking hold of him.

"I have a feeling that we are in a serious relationship, but I don't know if that's the case or if we're just having fun and messing around?" It comes out as a question, and I'm not sure what to respond. It feels so strange to have to tell him that we are in a committed relationship. I look into his clear blue eyes, and I can almost see the need for answers. Like it's somehow palpable.

"We love each other." The words are out before I can catch them, and I brace myself for his reaction. I'm not sure what I'm expecting, but when he brushes his hand over mine and says, "Good," I feel like I can finally breathe properly for the first time in days.

Chapter 6

Ethan

GOOD? WHAT KIND of response is good? Holy shit, I think I've just told her I love her—kind of. I've never said that before. Or maybe I have. For all I know I tell her I love her all the time. I'm not sure I even know how to be in love with someone. I don't think anyone except my mom has ever loved me before, but then again I wonder if she actually loves me at all? I mean, if she did she wouldn't have stood by doing nothing all these years as I struggle in this existence, desperately trying to impress a man that seemingly hates my guts, and likes to remind me of this with his fists. I shake the thought from my mind as I look up from my hand sitting on top of Blair's. The anxiety of thinking about loving her is causing it to tremble. She's watching me. Can she tell what's going on in my head right now? There's a hint of a smile on those perfect plump lips and I can't drag my eyes away from them. It's weird; my mind doesn't remember her, yet I'm pretty sure

33

my body does. I didn't mean to take her hand; it was a subconscious decision. I'm not a hand holder but there's no way I'm pulling away first. This feels too good, and it's threatening to make her smile.

"You're starting to freak me out."

Wait, what? I blink a few times trying to refocus my thoughts.

"Earth to Ethan," she laughs. The sound makes my body hum, and every single nerve is aware of her proximity and it's making me hard. I feel myself twitch before remembering that I'm wearing cotton pajama pants.

Shit.

I need to gain some control, think of something to kill my semi... Jackson's granny—yeah, that oughta do it. Jackson's granny naked on a cold day, Jackson's granny naked on a cold day, Jackson's granny naked on a cold day!

"I asked if you were allowed to leave the room. I thought we could go and get a coffee," she says, chewing on the corner of her bottom lip. It's undoing the work my little mantra was achieving.

I feel the corners of my mouth lift a little and something tells me I'd agree to go just about anywhere with this chick if she asked me.

"Why are you smirking? What are you thinking about?"

"Jackson's granny naked on a cold day," I hear myself answer.

I freeze in realization and immediately want to retract the words, but it's too late.

To say that she looks shocked would be an understatement. I panic and stand up from the bed. Her eyes ze-ro in on my junk and then she rears her head back looking completely mortified. Her jaw drops before she scrunches her nose.

"Oh shit, it's not what it looks like!" I practically shout. "Well, it is, but…damn, okay, so this is embarrass-ing. I was thinking about Jackson's granny to calm my dick down from you laughing."

Her features begin to smooth before morphing into amusement. She shakes her head a little and looks up at me, then back down to my crotch, before her eyes flick back up to mine. She's sporting a huge ass grin.

"At least someone remembers me!" she squeaks, and then lets out a full-blown belly laugh. Her head's thrown back as she clutches onto her stomach.

"I'd love to grab a coffee with you, but I'm gonna need a minute," I tell her, nodding towards the bathroom. "I have to go splash some water about and cool the hell down." I'm not shy, but I feel like a complete tool at the moment.

Her chuckles continue as she leans forward. "Shit, it hurts to laugh," she breathes, trying to rein in the weird giggle snort thing she's doing.

I smile at her in amusement. "Why does it hurt?"

She rubs gently at her side and then pulls her shirt up slightly. She's careful not to expose anything other than giving me a glimpse of the dressing covering part of her abdomen. "The stitches haven't healed fully from my sur-gery." She shrugs and then lets her shirt fall back into place.

My smile slips and my stomach plummets as I realize

35

that the whole time she's been in here, I didn't once think to ask if she's okay. The image of her holding a drip stand floats to the front of my mind.

Fuck!

Okay, so I'm failing at being a boyfriend right off the bat. I can hear my dad's voice in the back of my mind telling me what a selfish little prick I am.

"Blair, shit…I'm so sorry, I haven't even asked you if you're okay." I sit back down beside her on the bed and let my head drop. "What happened?" I motion to her stomach. "I know you were in the crash—are you hurt bad?" I ask, attempting to swallow the lump that's formed in my throat. I can feel myself break out in goose bumps. This girl elicits reactions from me that I have no control over. I don't know if I should love or hate that. What I do know is that I feel like crying and it's scaring the crap out of me. I don't do emotions, and I certainly don't do crying—not ever. I do numb, but I'm feeling anything but that at the moment.

"My spleen ruptured in the accident." She smiles, but it's sad. "I got off pretty lightly, unlike you and your dad." She sucks air in through her clenched teeth and then grimaces looking at me. I'm assuming she didn't mean to say the last part.

"I haven't heard anything about him yet." I try to pull off nonchalance, but I don't think it's working. I wonder how much she knows about my relationship with my dad? Would I have told her? I don't need to ask, though, because the look on her face somehow confirms that she knows.

"Do you want to know?" she asks as she pinches her top lip between her fingers waiting for a response.

"Honestly? I don't know if I care." I watch for her reaction. Waiting to see if I've read her wrong and she doesn't know about that aspect of my life.

She takes a hold of my hand and laces her fingers with mine; she draws her knee up and rests it on the bed then twists her body so she can face me.

"I can see you wondering...I know about him Ethan. You told me everything."

My stomach churns as I force myself not to look away. I feel ashamed, weak and pathetic all at once. I hate that she knows. There is nothing I wouldn't give right now for this whole situation to be reversed. Why couldn't I have forgotten about him and still remember her?

I sit mute: *what can I respond to that?* I open my mouth to speak before I've even processed what I'm about to say. Then I pause; she leans in and everything happens in slow motion as she places her lips lightly over mine. They're so soft. Damn.

She doesn't move them at all, just holds them in place, and I'm mesmerized. She's kissing me but it's not making out. In fact, it's not sexual at all. This kiss—it isn't really a kiss; it's an unspoken message. She's letting me know it's okay and that I don't need to try and make excuses. She moves her head back and looks directly into my eyes. She's so beautiful; her huge green eyes are fixed intently on mine. She looks unsure of herself, like she doesn't know if she's crossed the line and her head starts to drop along with her gaze.

Oh, hell no.

I take a hold of her face with both of my hands and bring her lips back up to mine. This time I'm the one in control and I kiss her like she should be kissed. The only message I intend to send is that I need to do this. I have to do this, just like I have to breathe. It's not a question of wanting; it's a necessity. I move slowly but deliberately, acutely aware of the sensation of blood rushing in my ears, my heart slamming painfully into my chest as she begins to kiss me back. Her hands rise and grip my wrists and I wince as pain shoots up my arm and I think for a second she's going to stop me, but she doesn't move my hands from her face. Instead, she holds on like she doesn't want to ever let go. It's painful, but I like it. I relish the sensation of her wanting my hands on her. I apply a little more pressure, and her mouth opens as I trace the seam of her lips with my tongue. Kissing her feels amazing. I've made out with plenty of girls but this is on another level, I can't get enough. Desire pools in the pit of my stomach as her teeth graze and nip at me, sending a shiver racing like lightning down my spine. I groan as a hot flush spreads across my chest and then slow my pace, placing a few chaste kisses at the corner of her mouth.

I finally find the willpower to pull away completely and look at her. We don't speak; there's no need to. I'm not sure I could even if I wanted to; I'm turned on to hell and completely confused with this whole situation. My chest hurts, but I think it's in a good way and I have to focus on calming myself down and trying to regain the breath she's just stolen from me. I'm still reeling in the sensations of our actions; it's never been like this before. She closes her eyes, and I watch her, waiting for her to do or say something—anything.

I know that this isn't our first kiss, or at least I'm assuming it isn't. But damn, it definitely feels like it to me. No kiss has ever tasted or felt that good. I'm trembling from head to toe, and that's certainly not something I'm used to. She's reduced me to thinking like a chick, over analyzing everything, I stare at her mouth that's all bruised from our kiss and smile internally. There's no wonder I made this girl mine; I feel like I could kiss her forever.

When her eyes finally open, they're glistening with unshed tears. I tense as I wait for her to get mad and start shouting at me. Worse still, she could reject me and ask me what made me think I could kiss her like that.

"Hi," she whispers, "I've missed you."

Thank you, god! I let out a long exhale.

"Blair," I pull her into my chest and rest my chin on the top of her head. I sigh as I squeeze and pull her tighter to me, inhaling her as I push my face into her hair.

"I know I don't remember us yet…but I'm pretty sure that I've missed you too."

Chapter 7

Blair

"MISS THOMAS," THE burly male officer states as I walk back into the stark, sterile confines of my room. One of the nursing staff had come to track me down; she'd interrupted Ethan and I to tell me that there were two police officers wanting to speak with me about the accident. It's the last thing I wanted to do as I was sitting wrapped up in Ethan's embrace, but I knew it was coming.

I offer a weak smile as I sit down on the bed nervously. My mom and a female officer enter the room seconds later; Mom perches on the end of the bed as the officer pulls the only remaining chair in the room closer to us. The feet drag and bounce across the floor, letting out a horrid screech that echoes through the eerie silence.

"Miss Thomas," the officer begins again. "I'm Officer Murphy, this is Officer Speight," he motions to his female colleague. "We'd like to ask you some questions regarding the accident you were involved in, if you're feeling up to it?"

"Sure," I answer, looking at my mom for confirmation. I'm not even certain why. She seems to sense my unease and shifts closer to me, placing her hand on my leg that's bouncing wildly. What is it about moms? One simple touch has the power of complete reassurance. I exhale and try to let go of the anxiety that's been steadily building in the pit of my stomach as I walked back from Ethan's room.

"Excellent; let's get straight to it, then," he says, taking a pen from his crumpled white shirt pocket. He proceeds to scrawl illegibly across the clipboard resting on his knee. His pant leg is bunched up and I can see the black and green sock he's wearing with a huge L for left on it. I like it; in a strange way it makes him seem more human.

The questions start thick and fast, hammering down like a torrent of rain from a pregnant grey storm cloud. I'm interrogated for over two hours about every single aspect of the accident that I can recall. Why were we in Arizona? What happened at the bar the night before? I have no qualms about telling the officers that Frank stopped the car in the middle of the road to pick a fight with Ethan. My mom sits quietly by my side with a pained expression as I retell the argument Frank and Ethan were engaged in when the trucker hit us.

I'm exhausted by the time the officers finally relent and decide to leave. I'm told that they will be 'in touch', and they'll be speaking to Ethan and Frank in due course. My blood runs cold as I realize that it's yet another promise that I've not kept. I promised Ethan that I wouldn't tell anyone about the situation with his father. I sang like a canary once Officer Murphy asked me to elaborate on Ethan and Frank's argument. Both officers sat staring at me and then glancing at each other, as if they were in some silent conversation while Mom kept squeezing my knee. I'm not sure whether it was in reassurance or sadness over what I was confessing. Once I mentioned the abuse the questions came faster. I got the feeling that they didn't believe me and it was frustrating as hell. Why would I lie?

Apparently the truck driver had died of head injuries at the scene. I'd been told he hadn't made it, but didn't know how or why until now. I remember seeing him on his cell shouting for help covered in blood. I squeeze my eyes tight and try to remove the image. The cops said he'd been talking to his wife on his cell phone when he hit us. Turns out the truck had veered slightly without him realizing. If we hadn't been stopped in the road like sitting ducks, we'd more than likely have been able to swerve and avoid the whole thing. They didn't say that, but I know it's true. I could have done without knowing he was on his cell to his poor wife. I'm pretty sure that I'll be revisiting that little piece of information in my dreams tonight. I can't imagine how awful it must have been for her to hear everything play out over the phone and not be able to do anything. The thought makes me shiver.

The officers leave the room, the soles of their shoes squeaking down the hall until finally they fade and silence descends once more. Before I can breathe a single word to break it Mom stops me.

"Why on earth did you not tell me what was going on, Blair?" She crushes me to her chest as she shakes her head over my shoulder chanting, "That poor boy," over and over. My eyes fill as I realize that all I've accomplished by keeping Ethan's secret is letting this whole situation escalate to where we are now. If I'd done the right thing and told somebody sooner, this wouldn't be happening. *Why do all the promises I make end up hurting?*

"Sweetheart, I need you to tell me everything, okay? And we need to speak to Moira, too."

I tense instantly and pull away from her embrace. "Moira knows. Well, not about the argument and the crash, I'm guessing, but she knows about the abuse."

I've never seen my mom look so horrified before. She drops down onto the bed and shakes her head as if she can't quite comprehend what I'm telling her.

"She *knows*?" she asks in disbelief.

"Yeah," I sigh. "A few weeks back, Moira told Ethan that she wasn't his biological mother. He had no clue. She told him that she had no legal right to ever be able to take him away and that she was too scared of Frank to do anything. That's why she let it happen." I feel the prickly cold remains of the tears I didn't know were falling bite against my cheeks as the air conditioning unit kicks in. I shiver and wipe my face. I want to curl up on the bed and pretend this isn't happening. My stomach aches, my head throbs and my heart hurts. Mom's sitting in stunned silence as I climb into the middle of the bed and curl up, hugging my knees into my chest. I tug at the blankets that have been made with military tight precision until they loosen and I can pull them over me. My stitches are wrenching from the awkwardness of my position and I welcome the discomfort; I'd gladly take this pain over the feeling of guilt that is consuming me.

"I'm sorry," I whisper.

"What are you sorry for, honey?" Mom asks moving closer and stroking the hair back from my face.

"For not telling you, for not telling anyone. I'd convinced myself that I was doing the right thing. That I was protecting him, but all I was doing was protecting Frank. I pushed all the bad things I knew were happening to the back of my mind. Then I made a promise to him that ultimately I knew I could never keep. How could I have done that to him? I'm so angry with myself for staying quiet as long as did." I sniff and move my glasses so that I can wipe my eyes on the sleeve of my shirt. "I'm confused Mom; I'm mad that I made that promise, but at the same time I'm upset that I broke it too."

"Oh, Blair." She draws her legs up and spoons me as we both lie on my hospital bed sobbing, her for my pain and me for Ethan's.

ele

I wake to the sound of a heated conversation. My mind is hazy from sleep and my eyes feel puffy and hot from crying. I sit up stretching and assess my surroundings. I'm alone in my room, but I can hear the muffled tones of my mom's voice. I look down at my phone charging at the side of the bed for the time. It's 5: 27 pm—I've only been asleep a little over an hour. I slide ungraciously off the side of the bed like a sloth and drag my feet across the room in a true zombified saunter, following my mom's voice. The door is cracked slightly, and I stop when I recognize who she's speaking to—Moira. I debate whether or not to stand and eavesdrop on their conversation but then I think better of it. I don't like the idea of people listening in on my conversations, and I imagine that they are the same.

"Mom?" I say loudly, alerting them to the fact that I'm about to interrupt whatever's going on. I open the door to find them both in tears.

My stomach plummets to the floor dragging my heart with it as all the different possible scenarios of why they could both be crying flood my thoughts. Ethan's the only thing that makes sense.

"What's wrong? Is it Ethan? Oh, no…it is, isn't it?" my voice wobbles and both women rush to speak.

"No!" The pair blurts out in unison, and I almost want to fall in relief. I lean into the door for support and let out an audible sigh.

"What's wrong, then? Why are you both crying?" They share a look before standing and ushering me back into the room. "We were talking about Frank," Moira answers, her voice shaky and quiet.

"Oh," is all I can manage to respond.

She lets out a pained sob as she jiggles her head and looks up towards the ceiling, attempting to control the flow of her tears by biting down on her lip and scrunching her eyes tight. I feel bad for her; she's in pain, but I still can't help the underlying stir of anger and resentment towards this woman. Every time I start to feel even a slight semblance of compassion for her, the nagging voice in my head whispers that she doesn't deserve it. I'm fighting an internal battle.

"Your mom was just telling me that Ethan had confided in you," she says between sniffing. "Blair, you will never know how grateful I am that he has you. That he's had somebody to talk to. We've never had that. He...he ..." Her sentence is cut short by a new wave of tears and my mom takes the few steps to reach her, ushering her into a chair while rubbing her back. I'm still standing. Motionless. I don't know what to do.

"We barely talk; he feels like I've failed him. I see it in his eyes every time I look at him. I need to make it right, and I have no clue how. I love him so, so much. You need to believe that. I've only ever loved him; I never wanted this life for him."

I can hear my own pulse echoing in my ears. "How's Frank?" I ask out of morbid curiosity. Her head snaps up, and Mom turns to look at me.

"He's not good, Blair," Mom answers.

"He was thrown through the windshield when you crashed," Moira begins. "The doctors said the impact shattered his C1 and C2 vertebrae. He's suffering from a cervical spinal injury; he's paralyzed from the neck down."

My mom had told me he was paralyzed when she first found out, but we didn't have any details. I thought maybe he wouldn't walk again. I had no idea his paralysis was from the neck down. I'm still standing in the middle of the room staring at Moira like she's speaking a foreign language. My first thought was to say how sorry I am to hear that. But I'm not sorry. I'm not anything; I don't know how I should be feeling. I think maybe I'm in shock.

"Are you okay, sweetheart?" Mom asks, looking concerned. "You've gone white as a ghost."

"I'm fine," I lie. "When are you going to tell Ethan about this?" I ask Moira.

"I'll tell him this evening, I guess. I just don't know what to say. The doctors have mentioned not to divulge too much about the accident. They don't want any excess stress; apparently it would be better for him to remember by himself. I'm worried that when I tell him about Frank, I'll be setting him back."

I take a seat on the edge of the bed and contemplate what she's saying. "You need to tell him, though; it's not right to leave him in the dark about this." Keeping things from him is what got us all into this mess in the first place. I don't say that out loud but she must know it's the truth.

"I will. Blair, I need to ask you something," she sighs. I immediately know I'm not going to like this particular 'something' from the look marring her face. I raise my eyebrows waiting for her to continue as she looks from me to my mom and then takes a deep breath before beginning.

"I know that Ethan told you about the conversation we'd had about me not being his natural mother." My heart sinks in my chest in anticipation of what I think I know is coming next. "He doesn't remember that conversation ever happening, and with his injuries and his dad, and everything else he has to deal with at the moment I just don't think he'd handle being told again. I'm hoping you can promise me that you won't tell him."

And there it is…that word, again. *I hate it.*

"I can't promise that, Moira. It's not fair," I say shaking my head. I can feel my mom's eyes burning holes into the side of my face. "I just…I can't lie to him."

"It's not lying," she interjects.

"It's not telling him the truth, either, though, is it? What happens if he starts to remember things, or asks me what he and Frank were arguing about in the car?"

"Blair's right, Moira. You can't ask that of her," Mom voices as she switches places and sits beside me so that we're both facing Moira now.

Her eyes are still brimming with tears, and she looks so worn down.

"I don't want you to lie to him, Blair. I just want you to not say anything to him about me not being his mom. If he asks you straight out, then by all means tell him the truth. All I'm asking is that if you do think he's remembering give me a heads up. I will tell him eventually, I just can't bear to put any added stress on him. In all honesty, I'm not sure if I'm even strong enough to tell him right now."

We sit in a weighty silence for what feels like hours, but I'm sure is only seconds in reality. I can't believe I'm in this situation again already. I want to tell her no, but then I know how broken he looked earlier today, and I think she may be right. I don't think he could handle this right now, and especially not if she's about to tell him that his dad's a quadriplegic.

"Fine," I mutter in a strangled whisper.

"What?" the pair of them reply at once, only Moira's voice sounds hopeful, and my mom's sounds almost stifled and disbelieving.

"I said, fine…I promise I won't say anything, unless he asks me flat out."

Mom shakes her head and gives Moira a look that quite clearly tells her she's not happy. Moira, on the other hand, looks like I just took the weight of the world from her shoulders.

We stay in my room for a little while longer, talking about Frank and what's going to happen next before Moira says she needs to get back to Ethan. I did plan on visiting with him again this evening but now I don't dare face him. Mom waits for Moira to leave before fixing me with the disappointed glower again.

"Don't say it," I put my hands up and look away from her as I climb into the bed. She sighs, picks up a magazine and begins leafing through the pages. She's accepting my decision, for now at least, and although I'm not even sure it's the right one myself, I love her for it.

Chapter 8

Ethan

From: Jackson
Hey man, how you feeling today? Your mom says you'll be home soon. The guys and I wanted to come visit you, but your mom's asked us to wait till you get back. Brie's filled me in on everything that's been happening. She texts Blair every 30 seconds for an update! Call me when you get a chance, bro.

I read the message and wonder why Jackson and Brie are even talking before I realize that I've obviously forgotten more than just my girlfriend. I begin to scroll through the fifty or so texts I've received from the rest of the guys over the last couple of days. They're all much the same, sending well wishes and asking about Blair and my dad. I don't feel like talking to anyone at the moment; I'm not sure my brain could handle it. I decide to send a text out instead. Besides, I doubt I could answer anyone's questions given that I still don't remember shit about the crash.

To: Jackson, TJ and 1 more...
Hey guys,
Doing good, should be outta here soon. Don't slack on band practice. I've screwed my wrist up pretty bad, I'm counting on you guys to pick up the slack and make me sound good at our next gig.

I hit send, and before I can even toss my phone back onto the bed, it starts going nuts with replies.

From: Drew
Good to hear you will be home soon. Not the same without you here, TJ's already trying to take your place as front man ;)

From: Jackson
We've got your back. Will call later

From: TJ
No offense man, but who cares about your wrist ;) Tell me about the nurses! Any hot ones willing to give you a sponge bath??? Send pics—of nurses, not you!

From Drew
TJ - You're a dick!

From: Jackson
The asshole's still on form, you ain't missing much here! Later Bro.

I smile down at the screen and for a fleeting moment, I actually feel like everything is normal until mom walks in and shatters the illusion. Her worried look is one I'm used to. She wears it a lot.

"You okay?" I ask, placing my phone down and giving her my full attention. There's a long pause and I know I'm not going to like whatever's coming next. I brace myself and wait for her to say what it is that's so blatantly bothering her. I can feel my shoulders begin to tense, and the silence is deafening. This is how it's always felt between us—strained and uncomfortable. I'm beginning to get agitated with this weird standoff we seem to have entered, and I'm about to tell her to just spit out what's wrong when she sits and decides to finally speak.

"I need to talk to you about your father, Ethan. He's in a bad way."

"So speak," I clip out. I don't mean to be short with her, but he's my least favorite subject and she knows it. I watch as she wrings her hands together, working up the courage to carry on. She's spinning her wedding ring around on her finger, something she does when she's upset.

"He sustained a cervical spinal injury, the first two vertebrae in his spinal column have been shattered by the accident." She pauses again, no doubt giving me a chance to absorb the information and ask questions. When I make no attempt to comment she elaborates. "Do you understand what that means, Ethan?"

"Not really, no," I tell her, shrugging my shoulders.

"He's paralyzed," she begins. "From the neck down.

The doctors have told me that the damage he's done means his skull and spine are not connected. They need to operate, but he's not strong enough at the moment and the surgery is dangerous."

Her eyes are glazing over as she holds back her tears. I can't figure out if they're meant for him or me. I know I should be displaying some sort of emotion, but I'm not. I feel completely numb. Her words are swirling around in the whirlwind that is my mind, but it's not stimulating any reaction and I know it's not normal. I pretty much detest my father; I have for as long as I can remember now, yet I'm not happy by this news. I've wished him dead on more than a few occasions, as messed up as that is, but paralyzed…that's somehow a fate worse than death. At least it would be for me. I can't think of anything in this world more cruel than being trapped inside your own body. I'm not sad either, though; my emotional state regarding my dad is about as damaged as his back, only there may be a chance that the doctors can help to fix that in some way; whereas, our relationship is so fractured, so broken, there's no putting it back together.

"What's the survival rate for the surgery?" I ask as a melancholic curiosity takes over. My voice shakes slightly as I speak; I clear my throat and look away, but Mom catches it. She moves closer and puts her hand on my shoulder, offering a comfort that I don't want and in truth, she can't really deliver. I stand, forcing her hand to drop as I move to look out of the window and her sigh is audible.

"From what the consultant told me, 50/50 at best."

I nod, contemplating her answer. The room feels colder than normal; the air conditioning unit is humming in the background providing an eerie theme to our conversation. I cross my arms to try and conserve some heat, and then let them drop immediately as the pain spears through my wrist. I'm no longer hooked up to the machines like before. I'd become accustomed to the steady, monotonous beeping and now that it's gone I miss it. The constant din gave me something to focus on other than reality. Now all I'm left with is the sound of my own voice in my head whispering that I might finally be free.

"Can I see him?"

She looks shocked at my request and eyes me carefully.

"It's just…I don't know; it doesn't feel real."

"I'll ask one of the nurses, sweetheart. I'm sure it will be okay, I'll go find out." Her voice is soft and low like she's talking to a little kid, or maybe like she feels sorry for me. I almost want to laugh in indignation. She must think this news is upsetting me. Doesn't she realize when it comes to Frank Jamison I'm dead inside? Any love I harbored for him was beaten from me long ago.

"Thanks," I huff as she walks out of the room.

$$\mathcal{elle}$$

"You answered! Dude I've been calling for days. How are you?" Jackson's voice echoes around the empty room as I place his call on speaker.

"Good, man. Sore and shit, but alive! I've been given the green light to come home tomorrow. Blair was told she'd be released today, Mom said, so I'm not sure if she'll be heading home yet."

"Yeah, Brie mentioned something about her being allowed home. How are you two?" His voice is laced with hesitation, and something else I can't place. Like he knows something that I don't.

"Honestly, it's weird. You know my memory is screwed at the moment, right? I don't know. I've spoken to her a few times and I have all these pictures and messages on my cell from her, but I can't remember a damn thing about her. It's pretty fucked up."

"Yeah, I can imagine. Look on the bright side, though …she's hot, and you get to do over all your firsts with her. First date, first kiss, first fu—"

"What the hell dude," I interrupt. "That's the most pussified thing I've ever heard you say, shit…you know you sound like Drew," I laugh.

"Fuck you, I do not sound like Drew!" I can hear his smile in the tone of his voice. "Anyway, how's your old man?" he asks tentatively. He's been my best friend since kindergarten and knows our relationship sucks ass. That's all he knows though, or, at least if it isn't, he never brought it up, and I'm thankful for it.

"Not good. I'm waiting on my mom to come back and let me know if I can see him…he's paralyzed."

"Shit…" I hear him blow out a long breath. "Like, what? He's not gonna walk again and stuff?"

"No bro, more like he's not gonna move again. He's a quadriplegic—can't move from the neck down. His spine and skull are not connected or something like that. He needs surgery." Saying it out loud doesn't make if feel any more real. The numbness is still firmly in place.

"I don't know what to say…that's, that's…Jesus, I

mean are you okay?" I think about his questions for a beat too long. "Ethan? You still there man?"

"Yeah, I'm still here. Look dude, my mom's about to walk back in so I'll talk to you later," I lie.

"Okay, later then. Call me if you need anything…at all, yeah?"

"Yeah," I reply as I end the call and lean back on the bed closing my eyes. I know full well that I won't call him or anyone else for help. I never have before in the last eighteen years, and I don't plan to start now. Blair's face flashes behind my eyes and I get a weird sensation in my chest. I don't know how or why, even, but suddenly I feel like if I did want to call anyone, I'm pretty sure it would be her.

ele

"You can go in dear," the lady at the nurse's station prompts as I hover at the door to my father's room. Mom smiles at her and opens the door, slipping inside quietly. I'm frozen to the spot; the door's cracked, and the room is dark. He's lying with tubes and wires protruding from every available patch of visible skin. There's a ventilator pipe, at least that's what I'm assuming it is, bandaged to his throat. His face is ashen; I can't make out his eyes clearly from here, just shadows that look to have sunken into dark pools of anguish against his uncharacteristically pale skin. The blood rushes in my ears, and I'm suddenly dizzy. I spin on my heels, fully intending to make a retreat when the lady from the desk appears at my side and leads me to a bench seat in the hall.

"It's a lot to take in. Do you want me to get you a glass of water?" She smiles.

"No, I'm good. Thanks. Just a little dizzy."

"You know, the wires and machines look scary and intense, but it's still him in there, under all of them," she offers. I don't tell her that's what I'm afraid of.

"The pipe in his neck…is that for him to breathe?"

"Sorry, I can't discuss that with—"

"I'm family," I interrupt. "He's my dad."

She gives me a sad smile, a pitying smile.

I hate pity.

"It's not a ventilator; it's a suction drain. Your father's lungs are filling with fluid, and the pipe drains that for him."

"Can he still talk?"

"He can. Why don't you go in and say hello? I'm sure he'll be happy to see you," she says standing. She's an older woman, small with greying blonde hair, and I feel like I should be the one helping her, not the other way around. I follow suit, and she pushes the door open to his room. Mom's standing at the foot of the bed with her head slumped into her shoulders.

"Get him out," he whisper-shouts and Mom's head spins around. She has tears streaming down her blotchy red cheeks.

"I said get him out of here!" he shouts louder this time. Mom's face crumples and I'm roused from my momentary paralysis by the sensation of being pulled back through the door and back out into the hall. The lady, doctor, nurse—whatever the hell she is—looks briefly horrified before her professionalism kicks in and her face smooths over.

"I'm so sorry," she says quietly. Mom appears, and the lady backs away. We both silently take a seat back down on the bench. I know the answer before I even ask the question, but it doesn't stop me from confirming it.

"He blames me?"

Her silence speaks volumes; I watch as she squeezes her eyes tightly shut. She looks as though she's in physical pain. I don't wait for anything else. I have my answer. I'm moving through the ward and barging through the main doors, sending them crashing into the walls, causing a thunderous boom before I let go of the breath I'm holding.

My numbness has morphed into something else.

Ice.

I feel a glacial bitterness descend as I move through the building as fast as I can. Suspended in a surreal state, I look down and realize I've taken my cell from my pocket and my thumb is hovering above the call button. I stop in my tracks, take a deep breath, and then another, and then another. My chest is burning and I feel like I can't breathe properly. I look back down at the display and don't think, I just press call.

"Ethan?" The sound of her voice is my oxygen. I draw in a long breath through my nose, dousing the fire in my lungs. I pause and close my eyes; my shoulders relax and drop.

"Hi, Blair."

Chapter 9

Blair

"ARE YOU OKAY?" I ask him. He's sitting on the floor with his back against the wall outside of the hospital. The hand that's not all bandaged up is cradling his head. I'm waiting on my mom to come and collect me, my things are packed up in my room and she's due back in the next twenty minutes. I told her I wasn't flying back home until Ethan was released, so she's gone to extend her hotel booking.

"Truthfully?"

"Yeah, truthfully." I smile.

"No."

The dejected tone of his voice pierces like a needle straight through my heart. I almost wince. I want to take away the pain that I can see he's in, but I have no idea how. I slide down against the wall positioning myself next to him and then place my arm over his shoulders, pulling him into my side as best I can without hurting his injuries.

He's so much bigger than I am, I'm stretched across him and the angle is pulling at my stitches but I don't care. I need to hug him about as much as he looks like he needs to be hugged.

"What happened?" I'm pretty sure it will have something to do with his dad. Moira had said she was going to speak to him about Frank; I should have gone to his room earlier to check on him, not avoid him like I have been. I was so consumed with thinking I might let something slip out about Moira, it didn't occur to me that he might need me. The realization leaves a bitter taste in my mouth. I'm beyond disappointed in myself. His head tilts so that he can look at me; his sad blue eyes are searching mine. He's looking so intently at me, almost like he's studying me and his gaze is penetrating. I feel a gleam of hope spark in the pit of my stomach while for a brief moment I'm sure he remembers who I am, remembers us. But then he blinks and looks away and I feel the glimmer of faith I'd pinned on that one tiny look burst like a bubble and dissolve to nothing.

"My dad blames me."

I bolt upright and drop my arm from his shoulders, pushing him away so I can see his face clearly. I can feel my eyebrows bunch together and my glasses slip a little on the bridge of my nose.

"What? Of course he doesn't. Why would you even think that?" I ask pushing my glasses into place as his lip quirks slightly and he lets out a bemused laugh.

"Trust me, Blair, he blames me. I went to his room earlier. Mom told me about his condition. I'd barely gotten two feet inside the door before he was shouting for me to get out."

My mouth must have fallen open because he flashes me a quick smile and places his finger under my chin and pushes my jaw back up. In any other circumstance this would embarrass me, but I'm too stunned and confused to feel anything other than amazement at the moment.

"I need you to tell me something, okay?"

I can feel the blood drain from my face as he looks at me waiting for me to answer. Goosebumps erupt under my shirt and my stomach drops as I swallow the knot in my throat.

"Okay, what?"

"The accident." He shifts his position and is sitting directly in front of me now. His legs flank my own as I pull mine up to my chest and hug them tightly. "Was it my fault—did I cause it?"

My skin prickles and a cold shiver shoots like a bolt of lightning down my spine. "What do you mean? Of course it's not your fault," I rush to answer, almost unbelieving that he could even entertain such a thought. He exhales loudly as a look of relief washes over his features.

"Ethan, you did not cause that accident! There were a number of things that happened that contributed to the outcome, but it wasn't your fault; you need to believe that, okay? You're not to blame."

He looks at me as though he's about to ask what I mean, but I move onto my knees and envelope him in a tight embrace. I push my face into the crook of his neck; the smell of him invades me. He's like my own personal tranquilizer, soothing me as I mumble into his shoulder that it's not his fault. I know he hears me when his arms snake around my waist and pull me in tighter.

"You'd tell me if it was though, right? You wouldn't lie to me?"

I assume that he can feel my anxiety as it begins to build, because he holds onto my shoulders and moves me away from him, fixing me with a stare.

"I can trust you to tell me the truth…right?"

I gather my wits and clench my fists as I try and sit a little taller. "You can trust me," I answer. *Why does this feel like a lie?* I hate Moira right now.

"Good," he whispers drawing me back into him and then standing us both up.

"So, girlfriend." He smiles and nudges my arm. I can't help but smile back.

"So, boyfriend," I reply, arching my brow as I wait for him to carry on.

"Shit, that sounds weird! Want to go and get a crappy hospital coffee with me before your mom collects you? It can be our official second first date?"

"Second first date?" I snort.

"Oh god, tell me I at least took you out on a date before tricking you into being my girlfriend? Or…wait, I didn't sleep with you and then you just decided that we're together did I?"

I feel my mouth drop open again at the audacity of the question. I'm contemplating how inappropriate it would be to junk punch him right here and now when the low timbre of his laugh rumbles from his chest and spills out into the stillness. I love that sound.

"Joke, Blair."

"You're a dick, Jamison," I retort in mock exasperation.

"You're kind of cute when you're offended," he smirks, looking down at me.

My heart squeezes excitedly in my chest as I bask in the compliment.

"You're forgiven," I grin back at him.

"That's good," he flashes his dimples and takes a step back. "Because I've just realized that I have no cash on me so you're gonna have to pay for this date," he winks, grabs a hold of my hand and starts walking back into the hospital, pulling me along with him. His strides are longer than mine and I'm almost skipping behind him, like a little child trying to keep up with a parent. Our arms are outstretched and he smiles and slows for me to catch up. It's then that it hits me just how much I've missed him.

ele

"You know my coffee order?" he asks in a perplexed tone as I place the vanilla latte down in front of him. He's sitting in the back of the hospital coffee shop by the window. Darkness is slowly descending outside, casting shadows throughout the deep red room. You could almost forget we're sitting inside a hospital if not for the two other patients across the room wearing pajamas and sipping their drinks. No doubt they're enjoying the smell of ground beans over alcohol wipes. I know I am.

"Of course I know your coffee order," I tell him, shrugging my shoulders and taking a seat opposite him.

"Huh…don't think I've ever had anyone know that." He nods and picks up the mug, taking a tiny sip.

"I know more about you than you realize," I smirk.

"Why do I get the feeling that I should be embarrassed?"

I let my head fall back and let out a completely undignified snort laugh. He's watching me, amused, as I cover my mouth to mask the noise. "You've done some pretty embarrassing shit," I muse.

"Really? Do you not know who I am? You must have forgotten that I'm in a band. I'm the epitome of cool." He smirks, taking a large gulp of his drink.

I splutter behind my hand and shake my head. "Oh my gosh…ego much! You have done so many embarrassing things I can't even name them all. In fact, I will name one." I shuffle and sit taller in my seat. "You Googled how to avoid premature ejaculation when we first started dating," I deadpan.

Coffee spurts from his mouth at breakneck speed, spraying over the table and dousing my face and shirt. The look on his face mirrors my own shock before it morphs to mortification. I burst into laughter and he quickly follows, his eyes glazed he's laughing so hard, and fires napkins at me from the dispenser while trying to clean his chin.

"Smooth!"

"I didn't say I was smooth, I said I was cool," he chokes out.

"That's just been added to the list, by the way."

"Ha! I don't believe you," he says, crossing his arms loosely over his chest and leaning back on his chair. "There's no way I would have Googled that. I don't have problems in the bedroom department, Princess."

I freeze mid-wipe and drop the napkin from my face.

"You called me Princess." I smile, and he looks confused.

"You always called me Princess. I can count on one hand the amount of times you ever called me Blair."

"Oh, um…" he pauses momentarily and scratches his chin. "It just feels natural to call you that. I'm not sure if it's a memory. I don't know, I guess I can't explain it…" he trails off.

"Don't worry, I just missed hearing it is all, it's nothing. Anyway, you totally did Google it. When I saw your search history you tried to blame it on Jackson."

He nods in contemplation. "Okay, now that sounds like something I'd do. You know this hardly seems fair." He motions between us. "Teasing the poor amnesia patient. I'm sure I know a ton of embarrassing stuff about you; just wait till my memory comes back…you'll regret poking fun at me then."

I finish wiping down my shirt and ball the napkins up, tossing the soggy beige pile onto the table between us.

"Ooh, Mr. I'm So Cool I'm in a Band…is that a threat?" I ask narrowing my gaze at him.

"No, Princess…it's a promise."

Chapter 10

Ethan

THINGS TO CHALK up as completely fucking mortifying:

#1 Asking the hot as hell chick that's supposedly your girlfriend out for coffee, only to realize you haven't got your wallet.

#2 Doing this after calling said hot chick to offload your problems like a total pussy.

Then, to add frosting to the damn cake of shame that you've just baked…

#3 Spitting the coffee that she had to buy you in her face.

When the hell did I turn into a complete moron? I'm contemplating calling Jackson and asking him if he knows where my game's gone, cause I sure as shit don't. I want to believe that it's the whole head injury thing that has me in knots, but I think that it's maybe just her. We seem to have an easy, comfortable banter. She's quick-witted and I like it; apparently so does my dick. Every time I'm around this girl she commands attention from my whole body. It's like I've reverted to being a thirteen year-old that's just realized girls have boobs. Speaking of which, Blair's wearing a seriously tight yellow t-shirt that has '$2 \infty + >$' stretched across her chest. It's taking some truly astounding willpower to not stare.

"Okay, my mom's parking the car. I need to head back to my room and collect my bags," she announces, pulling me from the X-rated daydream her boobs have me in.

"I'll come and help you with them. I'm a gentleman after all," I wink as she scoffs and scrapes back her chair from the table. There's a huge coffee colored stain covering her tits; I'm struggling with whether it embarrasses me or turns me on.

"What?"

"I can't believe I spat all over your...you know," I groan

"Neither can I, I had you pegged as a swallower!"

Her words color her cheeks, and I can't contain my laughter. I place my hand at the small of her back as I guide her from the coffee shop and electricity zings through my veins, coursing its way up my arm and leaving fire in its wake. *I wonder if she feels it too?*

She explains that she'll be staying in a hotel with her mom instead of flying home to Santa Maria, so we agree that once I'm released we'll collect my car and drive home. At the coffee shop she'd promised to fill me in on a few blank spots about what we're even doing in Arizona. I just hope my car hasn't been impounded, since I've basically abandoned it for the last week or so. I'm nervous as hell at the prospect of a ten-hour car journey with her, but weirdly buzzed at the same time. She's assured me it will be cool with her mom; I'm not holding my breath on that one, though. I'm assuming that my own mother will be staying here with Dad for some time yet. I don't see any reason to stay once the docs say I can leave. It certainly isn't like I'm wanted here; Dad made that perfectly clear. It suits me fine, the farther away from this fucked up situation I am, the better.

$$ele$$

"Well, Ethan, I've examined your scan results and gone over your notes and I'm happy to release you this afternoon. I have faxed over your records to a colleague of mine at Marian Regional Health Centre. Dr. Bishop is happy to take over your care plan. You've been scheduled an assessment with her in three days. The details are all down here."

"Thanks, Doc," I tell him as I reach and take the large manila envelope from his outstretched hand. I've been bouncing my heels waiting for him to come and approve my release all morning. I've never wanted to leave a place so much in my entire life. Mom thanks him for everything he's done whilst fixing me with an annoyed stare, alerting me to the fact that she's expecting me to do the same.

"Sorry," I drop the envelope on the bed and reach out to shake Dr. Moss's hand. "Thank you for everything," I tell him as I widen my eyes at my mom in a 'happy now?' expression. By the subtle shake of her head, I guess she's not placated by my efforts. *Whatever.*

"Are you really just going to leave?" she asks the second that we're alone.

"Yeah, why?"

"What do you mean, why? Ethan, your dad is in the ICU; he needs life-threatening surgery and you're just going to leave?" Her tone is laced with disbelief, but she doesn't sound angry; she sounds sad.

"Are you being serious right now? He hates me. Why would I stay—what for? He sure as shit doesn't want me here, or am I mistaken? Did I misinterpret the way he screamed for me to get out when I went to his room? Sorry Mom, but here is the last place on this fucking planet that I want to be. He blames me; you and I both know it. Nothing has changed. I'm always the one to blame. The only difference is that now he doesn't have the luxury of expressing his anger towards me the way he no doubt wants to. The way he's always done. So yes, Mom, I am about to *just leave*. I'm not waiting here and being used as a verbal punch bag, and for once, I'm not scared to walk away. Maybe that makes me a coward because I know that he can't just up and follow me, but honestly, I don't care. And if you had any sense, you'd do the same. You'd pick me and not him, and leave. But that's not you, is it? Never has been."

I watch as her shoulders sag, and she physically shrinks before me. Her face has paled, and her former look of disbelief has dissolved into shame.

"Ethan, I..." she lets herself fall like a ragdoll into the chair positioned across from the bed. Her sadness is palpable; she looks like a child in this scenario, not the parent. She raises her head and her eyes are red. "I can't just leave him in here."

The words fill the room from a whisper that hits me louder than if she'd screamed them into a megaphone. Only I'm not hearing, 'I can't leave him' I'm hearing, 'I can't choose you.'

I snatch the letter from the bed, and I'm out of the door just in time to hear her cry. *Good. Welcome to my life, Mom.* I make it a whole ten feet before I feel the hot bite of a tear slide lazily down my cheek. I wipe furiously at my eyes.

I. Will. Not. Cry.

I repeat the words low under my breath as I navigate the maze of corridors all painted in the same sickly pale green, no doubt chosen by some sadistic prick that hates his job and thought it would be a fun game to make every corridor look exactly alike to completely confuse us poor assholes that have to walk them. I finally find my way to the main exit and race through the large sliding doors as if I'm being chased. Maybe I am. Perhaps I'm trying to outrun the worthlessness and rejection that seems to never be more than two steps behind me. I emerge into the parking lot and squint as the bright midday sun casts a blinding glow through the cloudless Arizona sky. The heat is causing the air to ripple before me, dancing in waves as the blistering gleams bounce from car to car, prompting me to shield my eyes. I can't determine what hurts most: the dazzling light scorching my vision or the sting of holding back tears.

ele

I'm pulling up outside Blair's hotel as my cell vibrates. I reach down and retrieve it from my pocket to see she's messaged me.

From: Princess
Text me when you arrive. Our room number is 102; I'll come down to the lobby and meet you.
B xxx

I toss the driver a twenty and climb out of the cab. I had him pull over at an ATM on the way here. I run my hand through my hair and my wrist protests at the movement as I type out a reply with my good hand.

To: Princess
Outside now.
Ethan

I stare at the screen and debate whether or not to add kisses. I spend a few seconds putting way too much thought into it before deciding I'm a total douche and give myself a 'man the hell up and find your balls' pep talk. I hit send. Sans kisses. Obsess over it like a teenage girl at a Bieber concert and then send another text.

To: Princess

X 😊

She's already in the lobby by the time I've located my scrotum and made my way into the hotel.

"Hey you, how does it feel to be a free man?" she asks with a grin as I quicken my pace and stride towards her.

"Pretty good, actually."

I come to a halt just inches from her, completely invading her personal space, but I don't care about that at the moment. She's wearing yoga pants and a white tank, her hair's falling loose and wild across her shoulders and I'm close enough to smell the strawberry scent of what I'm guessing is her shampoo. It almost feels familiar. The reality of how close I'm standing dawns on me. My stance suggests that I'm about to greet her with a kiss, which I REALLY want to do, but I feel awkward. She's staring at me expectantly and I'm frozen. I don't know how to act in this situation. I know what I want to do, but as much as I want to grab and touch and kiss her until our lips are numb, I'm painfully aware of the fact that she knows I don't remember her, and I somehow feel like it would be taking advantage. I don't want her to think that I expect I can do whatever the hell I want to her because she's my girlfriend.

"Don't overthink it, Ethan," she smirks and I narrow my gaze.

"Overthink what?"

"If you should kiss me or not. You definitely should."

"Um, I wasn't thinking about kissing you." I wrinkle my nose and watch the color flood her creamy cheeks. The asshole in me loves that I can make her blush. Her eyes widen and she begins to stutter something before taking a step away and I lunge forward catching her around the waist.

"Where do you think you're going? It was a joke, Princess." My mouth cuts short any plans she had to form a retort.

My lips glide against hers, and my hands travel slowly from her waist up the full length of her torso before I move them to cup her face. She sighs, moving to press her stomach and chest closer to me. I'm acutely aware that we are standing in the middle of a busy hotel lobby, but kissing her is more important than acting in a socially acceptable manner. I'm not usually one for PDA but right now it's my new favorite thing. Someone coughs a little too loudly for it to be anything other than a cue that we need to move the floorshow to the room, except Blair and her mom are here together and I haven't booked a room. I'm fairly certain seeing us kiss passionately in the lobby isn't something her mom is going to be happy witnessing. I'm fighting a losing battle with myself to pull away when she solves my dilemma and breaks the kiss. Her face is still flushed as she breaks into a huge grin. It sends my pulse into a frenzy and I can feel my heart slam painfully against my ribs.

"That's how you should greet me from now on, by the way."

"That can be arranged, Princess."

"Good. Oh, and Ethan?"

"Yeah?"

"You might want to take your jacket off and reposition it somewhere else."

Wait, what? I look at her confused, and she glances down to my junk quickly, before meeting my eyes again. I feel my own cheeks flush with the realization that my jeans feel a hell of a lot tighter than they did before I kissed her.

"That's your fault," I tell her while moving my jacket to shield myself.

"Lead the way to your room. I need to use the restroom." I wink and follow as she walks ahead of me laughing.

Chapter 11

Blair

I'M SITTING ON the floor Indian-style as Mom lectures me on being safe, stopping when we need to, and not driving when we're tired. Ethan is in the bathroom and Mom has pounced on the opportunity to go over the same details that she's already drilled into me before Ethan arrived. To say she's not entirely on board with letting me travel home with him is the understatement of the century, but having discussed it to the point of wanting to strangle each other over our differences, she finally relented. We had a forty-five minute showdown wherein she point blank refused to let me drive home. She listed everything from the fact that we had both been in a crash and were perhaps medically not ready to operate heavy machinery (she'd die of worry), to flat out begging me to just fly back with her. After tears on both sides we finally agreed that she would take us in her rental car to go get Ethan's Camaro, and then he and I can go and see if our things are still at the campsite before we drive home. I get that she's feeling anxious; I am too. In truth, I'd be traveling back with Ethan regardless of whether or not I have her blessing; at least this way it's amicable.

Her speech is cut short by the sound of water powering against the bathroom basin, then shutting off abruptly seconds before the door creaks open and Ethan emerges rubbing his hands on a washcloth. We all stop and look at one another as the room falls silent.

"Am I interrupting something? I can leave you to talk if you'd like."

"No, Ethan, it's fine. I was just reminding Blair not to drive tired and to be careful. If either of you are feeling unwell make sure that you stop and call me. Just use your common sense, the pair of you, okay?"

"Yes ma'am," he replies and I snigger. Mom looks over and rolls her eyes at me.

"She hates being called ma'am. Makes you feel old, doesn't it, Mom?"

She leers at me, and then huffs, announcing that she's going to go fill the ice bucket. I stretch lazily and move from my position on the floor to the bed.

"So what's the plan then? You want to set off this afternoon, or first thing in the morning?"

"I don't mind," he answers through a yawn as he sits down next to me, leaning his back against the headrest.

"You seem pretty tired. I think we should go and collect your car, then come back here and set off tomorrow. Is that okay with you?"

"Sounds like a plan. Come here."

I scoot back on the bed, shuffling in a completely un-lady like manner and making it look like a whole lot more effort than it needed to be. He pulls me into his side like I'm a teddy bear, and sinks down until his head is nestled into the crook of my neck. He doesn't say a word as we sit in a comfortable silence, staring out of the floor-to-ceiling window that looks out onto the hotel pool. I'm not sure if it's thirty seconds or thirty minutes, but the sound of his soft tiny snores interrupt the silence. I smile as I rub my fingers through his messy hair, and he moans his appreciation and shifts, pushing his face further into my shoulder. Mom returns, takes one look at him and gives me a knowing look before depositing the ice bucket and retrieving her purse from the cabinet. She leaves without a word, and I thank her silently with my smile.

We stay huddled together on the bed for an hour before my mom returns and wakes us both from the best sleep I've had since arriving in Arizona. I stretch and rub my eyes underneath my glasses. I'm positive that I look a mess and quickly wipe at my mouth, worrying that I've drooled all over myself in my sleep. Ethan looks completely perfect as usual; messy hair and hooded sleepy eyes suit him—it's so unfair. His plain navy Henley is crumpled from sleep and hitched up slightly, exposing the taught tanned V that leads down under his jeans. I have a hard time not staring at it, even though my mom is standing in the same room.

"Okay guys, let's go find your car and then we can go for dinner. I spotted a nice looking restaurant while you two were snoozing."

"Excellent! I'm starving," Ethan announces and picks me up, placing me on the floor so he can move to get off the bed.

"What about you, Blair, honey? Are you hungry?" Mom asks.

I am, but not in the way she means and I'm pretty sure she wouldn't want to hear that. "I could eat."

"Great! Let's go, then."

An hour and a complete headache later, we pull up in Ethan's Camaro alongside the Honda Mom rented. My mom is one of those women that refuse to listen to the satellite navigation system, and just assumes that she knows better, even if it's somewhere she's never been before. We've made so many U-turns getting here it made me dizzy. The three of us walk into the little hole-in-the-wall Italian together, laughing that the car was only four miles away, yet it took us this long to collect it. I'm no athlete, but I could have definitely run to go fetch it faster.

ele

"What are you guys ordering? I can't make up my mind. I've narrowed it down to pizza or fettuccini. I don't want to make a decision first and end up with food envy when it comes out," I announce to the table in a whiney voice.

"You're so much like your father, you know? He would never order first, either."

I smile at her observation. I'll take that; Dad was awesome. I don't mind the comparison she's drawn; in fact, I like being told that I'm like him.

"I'm gonna go for the meatball pizza. No chance of food envy with that, right? Since you don't like them."

My head snaps to the side at breakneck speed, and I gape at him wide-eyed and open mouthed. *I must look so attractive!* I'm holding my breath and can feel my pulse picking up tempo, thrumming against my skin.

"What?" Ethan asks, looking perplexed at my reaction to his admission. He's obviously confused. Mom too, who regards me through furrowed brows like I've just grown a second head.

"How do you know that I don't like meatballs?" I ask cautiously, trying not to let the hope that's evolving inside me sprout wings and take flight.

"Um…you told me."

I smile, and it's too late; the hope is set free, fluttering through me like an autumn leaf being carried by the wind. I clench my fists to stop from clapping and resist the urge to bounce my knees in an effort to dissipate the adrenaline coursing through me.

"When did I tell you?"

"When I took you to…"

Confusion morphs into realization across his face as the penny drops. My smile is straining the muscles in my face—it's that wide.

"Holy shit! You told me the day we first met, and I took you to Marco's Pizzeria."

Mom is still looking utterly perplexed at our exchange.

"He remembers, Mom!" I almost squeal. My voice has climbed a few octaves and I sound like an overly excited toddler.

"Oh, that's fantastic," she beams. "Do you remember anything else?"

"I don't know."

Ethan looks to me, his concentration clear in the depths of his crystal blue eyes.

"I remember meeting you in the library at school. You had me acting like a complete stuttering fool," he says as he winks, and I melt.

"I remember us going out for dinner."

My whole body is tingling as I bask in the happiness that has made its first real appearance since the accident.

The accident…it's a sobering consideration that has an ugly apprehension sliding over me and cloaking me in dread as I formulate the question I'm about to ask. I'm under no illusions that it won't soberly dampen everyone's newfound excitement.

"Is that all that you can remember? Can you not recollect anything more? The crash, maybe?" I ask tentatively. His smile falters and his shoulders drop ever so slightly, but I catch the movement.

"No—at least I don't think so."

"Well, never mind honey. This is a start," Mom interrupts in her best cheery 'fake it till you make it' voice.

"I'm sure you'll start to regain the rest of your memory soon."

"Yeah, hopefully."

I feel a little bad that he has no idea what he's actually hoping for. I know with an unwavering sense of clarity that his memories of the crash will be an unwelcomed gift amongst the rest. I sit back quietly as I make a mental note to text Moira as soon as I can and let her know of the developments. I feel sneaky and I don't like it one bit.

Chapter 12

Ethan

I LIE ABOUT what I can remember. It isn't just meeting Blair and going to Marco's that I recall; I remember what transpired when I returned home. Being locked in the garage with my dad, the beating he delivered all because I'd forgotten I had plans to help him. I can hear him telling me what a useless, selfish person I am as if he were right here beside me, whispering it to me at this exact moment. I shudder, trying to dislodge the thought. I can't tell them this, it will only upset them and if I'm honest with myself, I don't want to say it out loud. It makes it too real. I was telling the truth about the crash though: I still have no clue as to what happened or why; all I know for sure is how frustrated it's making me. All this 'we don't want to cause any undue stress' bullshit is what's causing my stress. How ridiculously ironic. Surely everyone can see that! Whatever. If they don't tell me to my face, I'm sure I can manipulate some information out of them somehow. I've never had a problem getting what I want from women before; I don't see why I would now.

"How's your food, Ethan?" Susan asks taking a sip of her ice water. "You've hardly touched it."

"It's good, thanks. Guess I'm not quite as hungry as I thought." I push my plate aside and lean back into the booth. "I'm going to step outside and grab some air if that's okay. I have a headache." I shuffle across the seat and maneuver past Blair, who's studying me with a concerned frown.

"Want me to come with you?" she asks, already pushing her food away and wriggling her way around the circular booth.

"I'm good, Princess. Stay with your mom; I just want to clear my head."

I leave before she has a chance to reply, It's not that I don't want her with me, it's more that when she *is* with me she's all I can focus on and it's distracting as hell.

I make my way out to the front and lean against the rough red brick wall. The sight of traffic rapidly passing by makes me dizzy as it blurs into a continuous stream. My headache feels like a jackhammer beating behind my eyes. It's rivaling the worst hangover I ever had when I was fifteen and Jackson and I drank a whole bottle of his dad's whisky when his parents were out of town. The smell of exhaust fumes mingles with the aroma of the restaurant, lingering in the thick humidity of the afternoon. I'm standing here all of thirty seconds before I feel someone touch my arm.

"I told you I'm fine, Prin..." my words falter when I realize it's not Blair. "What are you doing here? How did you even know where I was?"

"I called Blair. She told me where you're staying, I was on my way over when I noticed you as I was driving by…look, I wanted to come and talk before you headed home."

"Fan-fucking-tastic! I thought we were done talking back at the hospital, Mom."

"Watch your language, Ethan," she clips with a hint off pissed-off tone to her voice. It's not often she gets like this with me. Probably because she feels like she has to be super nice to make up for everything she doesn't do, like put me before him.

"The doctors can't give me a definitive timeframe for when or even if your dad can be moved to a hospital closer to home," she begins. "I don't like the thought of you going back and being so far away."

I scoff at the suggestion that she gives a shit. "If it bothers you that much, Mom, you'd be coming home with me."

I huff out a disgruntled breath when she doesn't respond, sensing that this conversation is pointless.

"Look, I'm eighteen years old. I don't need babysitting, and I'll be fine on my own."

"You're not fine, Ethan, you're recovering from surgery. You have retrograde amnesia and heaven only knows the emotional trauma all this is causing."

She moves to place her hand on my shoulder and I step away sharply. The hurt is instantly evident in her eyes; her face falls and the part of me that isn't a screwed-up mess feels bad.

"That's the one I dislocated," I tell her, hoping she'll

accept it as the reason I don't want her comforting me. "It's still sore."

"Sorry," she says, shifting her weight on her feet.

"Listen, Mom. I've told you that I'm going to be okay. I have Blair and Susan if I need anything. Hell, if I get really desperate I can always call on Jackson. He's only around the corner from us; I can always get a hold of him if I have to. I'm set; you don't need to worry."

She frowns and then begins rummaging around in an oversized purse she's always carrying. I have no idea what could constitute the need to carry around a purse large enough to transport a small child. She squats on the floor and starts to pull out all of its contents one by one. Her cell, a notebook, what I'm assuming is a makeup bag, deodorant, a pack of tissues. I stare at her, getting more and more frustrated as she searches. A young couple walks past and the woman almost trips on all the shit Mom has laid out on the sidewalk. The guy is looking at us like we're crazy.

"Mom, what are you doing? Get up, you're embarrassing me."

"Oh, hush your mouth. I can't find—oh wait, here it is." She pulls her wallet from the bag and holds it out to me triumphantly. "Found it," she says, handing it over.

All that hassle. Why chicks don't just carry them in their pockets, I'll never know. I wait impatiently as she shoves all the crap she's just unpacked back into the purse.

"Right, that's better," she announces, taking the wallet from me and pulling out her Amex card. She hands it to me. "You know my pin, so use it for food, gas et cetera. Just don't go overboard with it."

I give her a surprised look. "Um, okay. I don't need it though. I have money."

"I know, honey, but I'd feel better if you used it. That's not an invitation to go and buy that new Fender, though." She half smiles. "Try to be responsible."

"Okay, look, I need to get back in there." I point my thumb behind me to the restaurant. "They'll be wondering where I am."

"Oh, okay. Ethan, honey, I just wanted to ask—how's your memory? Are things starting to come back to you yet?"

She asks in a strange tone, worried or nervous, may-be. It's only been a matter of hours since I saw her last. Why would she think anything had changed?

"No, not yet," I lie. I'm not even sure why, but I don't want to tell her the truth. She bites at the inside of her cheek and studies me for a moment. I think she knows I lied, but she doesn't call me out on it. There's an awkward silence as my mind is racing about why she would ask me that and then react so strangely. *How would she even know I was lying?*

"I'll let you get back to dinner." She moves closer and gives me a small, quick hug. It's about as unnatural as they come. We don't have a cuddly mother-son-rainbows-and-unicorns relationship.

"Bye, Mom." I make my way back into the restaurant as she shouts that she'll call me tomorrow. I don't acknowledge it; chances are I won't answer if she does. Nothing has changed from earlier. She's still choosing him, and I still hate her for it.

Chapter 13

Blair

WE ARE ON our way to the campsite, Ethan's driving, and I'm tucked up in the passenger seat, wondering why this feels so awkward. He's barely spoken to me since we finished dinner and collected his car from the seedy bar where we abandoned it. He was acting strange when he walked back into the restaurant. He didn't mention that he'd seen Moira, and I haven't brought it up because I didn't want him to question how I knew she'd seen him. I can't formalize a good enough excuse to tell him, and the truth—that I'm feeding her info on his memory so she can keep secrets from him—sits so badly with me that I'm sure he'd hate me. Why wouldn't he? I'm starting to. I need to talk to her when we get home. I can't do this; I should have just said no in the first place.

"You warm enough?" he asks as he fiddles with the dials on his dash. "You're shivering."

"I'm fine, baby."

"So we'll pick up our shit from the site, go get gas and head out, okay?"

It's more of a statement than a question so I simply smile and rest my head against the cool glass of the window, watching him as he studies the road ahead. Something is definitely bothering him.

According to my mom, someone from the site had called her while we were at the hospital. I guess they had noticed that we hadn't packed up and left when we were supposed to.

We make it to the campsite after what feels like the longest twenty minutes of my life. I hate how the mood keeps swinging from comfortable to awkward. The unsettled feeling I have is ramping up as we pack up our belongings and he still doesn't attempt to make conversation. I throw my bag into the trunk and my resolve finally snaps.

"Ethan, has something happened? Are you mad at me? You've barely spoken a full sentence to me at all in the last hour."

"Why would you think I'm mad at you?"

"I'm not sure," I shrug. "I just know something's getting to you, and you are not doing a particularly stellar job of hiding it." His eyes shoot up in surprise at my observation.

"You know, I think you may be the only person who's ever called me out on that. Not many people can read my moods like you seem to be able to."

I step up close to him and circle my arms loosely around his waist. The heat is radiating from underneath the soft worn cotton of his t-shirt and warms my wrists. I tilt back so I can see him more clearly.

"Yeah well, I'm not just anyone, and I know you. I know that when you're upset you get a little crease right here above your nose." I smile as I trace over the small indent before dropping my hand back to his waist. "I know that you drum your fingers on any available surface when you're feeling anxious. You hum without realizing it when you're relaxed, and I happen to know that if you smile genuinely, the dimple in your left check is deeper than the one in your right. I pay attention."

"You pay attention, huh?"

"Of course I pay attention, I—" He silences me with a kiss. Fire dances behind the ice blue of his eyes, and he's staring at me fiercely as his lips are pressed softly over mine. His intense expression is in complete contrast to the softness of his actions. The breeze chills the moisture on my lips. I shudder as he pulls away, and another chill races along my spine. I feel the ardor of his stare on my skin as his eyes map out every contour of my face, as if committing it to memory. Messy brown hair falls over his forehead, tickling my own as he moves forward again.

This time his eyes drift shut as he cradles my head in his hands and pulls me forward to meet his mouth. The warmth of his breath fans over my face and then his lips send electric pulses through mine as they move with a slow deliberation. I can feel my knees buckle, and I'm thankful he's holding my face because I'm certain I'd sink like a boulder, and land in a mass of boneless skin at his feet. I'm completely lost, stumbling further into the abyss of my affection for him. He doesn't even seem to know what he's doing to me. I move my arms from his waist and slide them between us, running them up his stomach and chest, squeezing them amid our tightly packed bodies, and finally bringing them up to cup his face, the same way he's holding mine.

He kisses me breathless, until I have no real conscious realization of where we are, or how long we've been standing here. Heat pools in the pit of my stomach as he pulls my bottom lip into his mouth and nips at it, dragging his teeth slowly over the flesh before releasing and placing tiny kisses over the bite. We finally break away, dizzied by the exchange, and he rests his chin on the top of my head, tucking me into his body like I'm an extension of him. It's exactly where I belong.

I listen to the erratic rhythm of his breathing as he attempts to catch his breath, inhaling slow and deep. My face moves up and down as its rests over his heart, mirroring his breathing. The smell of soap and something that is uniquely Ethan infiltrates my senses; coupled with my dazed mood from our kisses, it makes for an overwhelmingly heady combination.

"You make it impossible for me to stop kissing you—you know that, right? I can feel my chest burn, and my lungs scream for me to stop and take a breath," he smiles and I can hear it come across in his voice. "I know that I need to pull away, but I can't. I don't want to, and I'm sure I'm about to suffocate, but I don't care because it would be the sweetest way to die," he whispers. I feel his words in every part of me; my toes curl, my fingertips tingle and if it's possible for a person's whole body to blush, I'm betting that's what mine is doing right now.

"I bet you say that to all the girls," I say sarcastically

with a small grin.

He pulls away, pushing me back at arm's length while holding onto my shoulders. The sereneness of his expression morphs to ferocious passion. The wind is blowing strands of my hair across my cheeks and slapping them against the lenses of my glasses. I can feel my arms break out in goosebumps and I'm sure they have nothing to do with the gusts of wind that are slowly starting to pick up and everything to do with the way Ethan's looking at me right now.

"You are the first and last person I will ever breathe those words to, Blair." The seriousness to his voice sends a shudder racing through my body. There isn't a single ounce of doubt in his voice and my stomach tightens. I watch the calmness return as I respond in the only way I know how. I rise on to my tiptoes, place my cold cheek against the unshaved roughness of his, and tell him the only truth I'm certain of at this moment.

"I love you."

elle

We've been traveling for about an hour since stopping for gas. After the exchange at the campsite, Ethan's acting more like himself, although the telltale crease above his nose is prominently visible, mocking me that there's still something troubling him that he hasn't chosen to confide in me. I have no right to know every little detail about him, but it doesn't stop me from wanting them.

"My headache hasn't gone. Do you have any painkillers with you?"

I lean forward to reach into my purse strewn at my feet.

"Shit! Ouch! Crap that stings!" I fling back into my previously reclined position, the biting burn of my stitches pulling, and then easing ever so slightly as I reach under my shirt and attempt to rearrange the position of the dressing that's tugging at the sensitive skin around the wound. I wince as my cold fingers come into contact with the hot skin around the incision.

"What? Fuck, what's happened? What's wrong?" Ethan asks, jerking the car to the side of the road, panic clear in his voice as he comes to an abrupt stop. The action has me jolting forward in my seat and the seatbelt locks, stopping me from being propelled forward, but tightening across my stomach in the process and causing even more pain.

"Blair, what's wrong?" he shouts, pulling me from my thoughts of how much this sucks right now.

"Relax, baby, I'm fine. My stitches just pulled," I manage to grind out as I'm frantically trying to unbuckle myself and release the pressure over my tummy.

"Here, let me…there, is that better?" he asks leaning over and releasing the buckle for me. I let out a huge sigh of relief as I try to straighten my body out in the cramped confines of the Camaro.

"Damn, you near on just gave me heart failure! You sure you're okay?"

"Yeah," I lie. The pain is making me feel nauseous, but the look of panic in his eyes is making me feel worse.

"I didn't mean to scare you, sorry. The pain just caught me off guard."

"Princess, you don't have to apologize."

"I have painkillers in the front pocket of my purse. Can you reach them for me? I think I need to pop a couple of them suckers now, too."

He regards me with a concerned look before retrieving the little white container of pills. "Here," he passes them over with a bottle of water he has rested in the side of his door.

"You want a couple?" I ask as I pop the lid and shake two chalky white capsules into the palm of my hand.

"Yeah, but I'm gonna find us a motel first. I can't concentrate with this headache, and you're not exactly in a position to drive," he says, rubbing his temples. "Plus, let me see those." He reaches out and takes the bottle from me. "Yeah, thought so. The warning states that they'll make you drowsy. Can't take them and then drive," he frowns.

"We don't seem to have gotten very far. At this rate it will take us a week to drive home."

"You're saying that like it would be the end of the world to spend a week stuck in my car with me," he laughs.

"Um, there are only so many car games I can play before I want to murder someone," I grin as his eyes widen.

"Okay. Mental note to self: car games are not Blair's thing."

"I don't mind playing a few, but when we're scraping the barrel and you're inventing games like, What Dinosaur Would You Be? I get a little crazy."

"What Dinosaur Would You Be? Huh. I have that weird déjà vu thing going on. We've played that, right?

And FYI, it sounds like it would be an epic car game."

"Did you really just say FYI?" I giggle. "You sound like Brie, and yeah, we've played it."

"Okay, so first you make out like it's a bad thing to be stuck in the car with me, and now you're telling me I talk like a girl. Are you always this complementary?" he asks with a wink. My god, I love it when he does that. I sigh and his dimples make a welcomed appearance.

"Are you having dirty thoughts about me?"

"WHAT!" I scoff, "No, not at all."

"Shame, I'm having all kinds of kinky thoughts about you."

I feel the heat spread from my cheeks, straight down my chest and shoot south.

"Shut up," I laugh and push at his side.

"What? I'm serious. It's the weird little snort you do when you laugh," he says nodding his head and biting down on his lower lip. "It's like it has a direct dial to my di—"

"Oh my god! Shut up!"

"Why? It's true!" he says, grinning from ear to ear.

He knows he's embarrassing the hell out of me, and he's enjoying it. Maybe I should let him carry on, my pride can take a knock if it keeps that gorgeous smile on his face.

"Okay, enough with the snort fetish, pervert…let's get to a motel."

"See, you are having dirty thoughts. And now you're trying to get me to some seedy roadside motel, so you can have your wicked way with me. Admit it."

I want to act all cool and calm, but even though he's

mocking me, the suggestion of a motel has totally got my mind in the gutter.

"I thought you had a headache."

"I do, but research shows that sex actually helps get rid of them—something to do with the endorphins released."

"You really are a perv!" I smile.

"Takes one to know one. Besides…you love it."

"Calm it, Casanova. Let's go find a room."

"And you're the one calling me a perv."

I shake my head and laugh as he checks his mirrors and pulls back out onto the road. He's right, though. Now that he's brought up sex that's all that's running through my mind. That and the fact that I'm in no fit state for him to see me sans clothing. I'm hoping like hell that I packed a razor and I'm running a mental inventory of all the things that should have been in my bag that was left at the campsite. My perfume, the girly underwear I packed, the bumper pack of protection, and that's when it hits me. I remember what else was packed—Em's letter. The butterflies and eager anticipation from moments ago are demolished instantly by the weight of my heart tearing through my chest as it crashes down to my feet. Now all I can think about is what if he remembers.

Chapter 14

Ethan

PRESSURE IS STEADILY building behind my eyes; I keep pressing my finger to my temple, hoping that I've suddenly developed a magic touch that will heal a migraine with a simple tap. I've only had a migraine once before, to my knowledge. It was after my dad had hit me in the stomach. I was fourteen and I remember stumbling backwards and hitting the back of my head on the corner of a bookshelf. The pain lasted for three whole days; Mom wanted to take me to the emergency room to make sure I hadn't fractured my skull or something. He told her I was milking the attention she was showing me, that it was probably a ploy to get out of going to school and that I was a lazy son of a bitch for staying in bed. I couldn't see straight, and the light hurt my eyes, which is kind of how I'm feeling now.

"This looks okay, right?" I ask, pulling into the parking lot of a Motel 6.

"Sure, I'm easy. I'll sleep anywhere."

"That's not something a guy wants to hear his girl-friend say," I grin.

"Are you kidding me? I thought that's exactly what a guy would want to hear."

I smile and bob my head at her, instantly regretting it when a wave of nausea follows the throbbing that the movement causes.

"Come inside with me. I'm not leaving you out here on your own," I tell her, getting out of the car and making my way over to where the red neon sign flashes Vacancies. She jogs up beside me capturing my hand in hers as we go to book a room.

elle

"This is nice," she grimaces, taking in the seventies decor and brown and green swirly carpet tiles. I toss my duffle bag on the king size bed and pull the comforter back.

"Sheets are clean; that's always a good sign," I smirk.

"Bathroom looks clean too!" she shouts as she closes the door behind her.

I let myself collapse on the bed and toe my boots off, letting them fall with a loud thud. The only light in the room is coming from a dirty orange-colored lamp; it's highlighting the dust particles streaming in from where the long green drapes don't quite meet in the middle. By any-one's standards it's dull in here, but there's still enough luminescence to have me placing my arm over my face to try and shield it. I hear the door crack, and then the bed dips where Blair sits by my legs.

"I'm retracting my last statement."

"Huh?"

"The bathroom…it's not clean. Well, the bathroom itself isn't dirty, but the water out of the taps runs a rusty color for at least twenty seconds before morphing into a kind of cloudy chalky-colored stream. Just don't drink any, okay?"

"Noted. Hey, can you find me a couple of your pills now?"

"Your headache still bothering you?" She frowns as I lower my arm and squint at her.

"Yup, the doctors warned me I might have headaches though. I guess I didn't realize how intense they might get."

I swallow the pills she passes me without a drink, and stretch out on the bed after flicking the switch off on the lamp.

"You mind if we keep the lights off? It's kind of bothering me."

"Not at all. Do you want me to keep my distance? I hate being fussed over and talked to when I'm feeling ill."

"I'll take all the fussing you want to give, Princess," I tell her as I reach out and pull her down beside me, tucking her under my arm. My shoulder and wrist ache, but the feel of her pressed up against me is enough to stop me from moving.

"You realize that you neglected to tell me what's wrong earlier. Want to tell me now?" Her voice sounds muffled as she speaks into my chest, where her head rests.

"It would be quicker to tell you all the things that are

right, instead of detailing everything that's not." I pause, wondering what possessed me to answer like that. Now she'll definitely push for answers. I watch as she rolls onto her stomach and shuffles trying to find a comfy position before she props her head up on her palms. She's no doubt making herself cozy, anticipating that I'll elaborate. So that's what I do. I take a deep breath and hit her with it.

"Where do you want me to start? My dad needs life-saving surgery, except he's too weak to undergo it at the moment, and instead of being worried about the fact that he might not pull through, I'm nervous that he will. How screwed up is that? I mean, what kind of person thinks like this?"

She doesn't skip a beat in answering. "The kind who's had to deal with a lifetime of cruelty that's who. Baby, if you ask me, what you're feeling is probably an entirely valid and reasonable response. He has been such a negative force in your life that it's understandable you would want it to end."

"That's the thing though, Blair; I'm not wishing for all of the crap to stop, for him to miraculously decide that he doesn't hate me anymore. I'm wishing him dead. That's not normal, Princess, it's fucked up by anyone's standards. I don't expect you to tell me it's okay, I already know it's not." I cough, trying to dislodge the pitiful whiney tone my voice has adopted. That taste of disdain is acrid on my tongue. "You want to know what freaks me out the most, though?" I ask as I push myself into a sitting position, resting my back against the cold hard panels of the wooden headboard. I figure I'm on a roll; I need to get this out now or I'll never say it out loud.

"What?" Her glasses slip off the bridge of her nose from the frown marring her face. I reach forward and push them gently back into place, mesmerized momentarily by the brief touch of her soft skin against my callused fingertips. Her eyes are glinting like emeralds as she waits for me to continue. I exhale, causing a loose strand of her hair to dance across her forehead.

"It's not feeling any different. I've ambled along numbly for as long as I can remember, shutting everything off so that I don't have to deal with whatever he decides to throw at me. What happens if he dies and I'm still like this? Just an empty vessel existing day by day, anesthetized inside."

I observe the moment my words sink in; pain—or perhaps sympathy—moves across her face, and the room suddenly feels too small; the space between us thick with tension.

"I think maybe something is broken inside of me, you know? Like the part of me that used to care about him—hell, the same part that used to care about me, even. I've repressed it for so long, what if it never comes back? I have these weird thoughts, kind of like daydreams. I can be tuning my guitar, or playing a piece on the piano and zone out. Suddenly I'll be with my dad, he's beating my ass and I'm letting it happen, but he doesn't tire like normal. He keeps whaling on me until I lose consciousness, but I can make out that he's shouting at me, 'Why won't you just die?' Then I think to myself that maybe it would be better if I did."

It's not until the sound of her sob escapes into the quiet room that I truly realize what I've just said. I can't decide if it's shock, worry or horror in her stare; maybe it's all three.

"Don't cry, Princess, I'm sorry. I shouldn't have said all that. I'm tired, I guess." Her tears are hot against the pad of my thumb as I run it over her wet cheeks.

"Ethan...I," she can't manage to verbalize the rest of her sentence, her cries are making her breath stutter.

"Hey, shush...I'm a dick. I don't even know why I said that. My head hurts, and I'm feeling sorry for myself. Ignore me."

"Do you really believe that? Please tell me you don't think you'd be better off dead." Her face is turning blotchy as she's furiously trying to rein in her emotions. I hate that I've made her this upset. *Why the hell did I think telling her this would be a good idea?* I know better than to shoot my mouth off—nothing good ever comes of it.

I shake my head in response and pull her onto my lap. Her legs straddle me as I pull her tightly to my chest, resting my cheek against her hair and burying my face in the soft waves as I make shushing noises softly into her ear. I rub small circles into her back and feel the shudders vibrate from her chest, straight through into my own.

Her grip on my t-shirt tightens and the realization that I don't know what to do to make her feel better has me hitting a new low. It terrifies me how connected I feel to this girl. Watching her cry is infinitely more painful than anything the asshole has ever doled out. Her warm tears slide over me and dampen my skin.

"Blair, look at me." I wait for her to crane her head back and then move my face down to hers, covering her lips with mine. I can taste the salt from her tears on my tongue, and it's a bitter contrast to the sweetness of her lips. It's not exactly a selfless act; I'm trying to make myself feel better as much as I am her. The kiss is slow and passionate. Her lips bounce from mine every time her breath judders. My fingers move deftly under the hem of her shirt and dig into the soft skin above her pants. I can feel her goose bumps erupt under my touch, and the asshole inside of me loves the response I evoke, even though I'm the one responsible for the hurt she's experiencing right now. What started out to be comforting is now morphing into a desperate plea. My scalp prickles as I revel in the feel of her hands pushing through my hair; my headache feels like a dull memory as she grinds against my lap. I swing my legs off the bed and stand, holding her in place with my good arm as she crosses her ankles behind my back to keep from slipping.

"Princess," I mumble trying to speak without breaking the contact of our mouths.

"Hmm."

"You need to tell me to stop." *Kiss.* "I don't want to take advantage." *Kiss.* "When you're upset." *Kiss.*

She presses herself harder into my chest and squeezes her legs.

"You're not; please don't stop."

It's all the encouragement I need. I lay her down on the bed in my spot and position myself over her. I'm shaking with the effort it takes to not place my weight over her stomach, while trying hard to hold myself on one elbow—the other is too weak to take the strain.

Her eyes are still glassy; her cute button nose has turned red, and her cheeks are tear-stained. I've never seen anyone look so perfect. I don't know what she sees in me, or why she wants to be with someone so broken, but I couldn't be more grateful.

"I love you." It's the truth, just like there are twenty-four hours in a day, or the earth is round. It's fact. I can't remember much about her, but I know with an unwavering sense of certainty that I love her. How could I not?

"Ditto."

I don't give her a chance to say another word as I claim her mouth once more. My hands are slowly pushing at her pants, trying to guide them and her underwear over her ass and down her smooth, cool legs. She pushes up from the bed to let me drag them down further, and when I've pushed them as far as I can reach with my arm, I use my foot to shove them over her ankles and kick them to the bottom of the bed. My hand travels down her waist and stops at the apex of her thighs. I'm dizzy and nervous and a little petrified, but excited at the same time. I hesitate, deciding if I should unbutton my jeans or take care of her first. I've somehow lost all of my courage; I don't normally need to second-guess this type of thing. Her tongue plunges into my mouth, and I decide that I need to lose the jeans and fast.

Chapter 15

Blair

MY HEAD IS swimming with his confession. He daydreams about dying. I don't know how to process what
he's told me. I can taste my tears as they mingle with his
kisses and I want nothing more than to focus on the feel of
him hovering over me, kissing me, loving me, but it's
tainted with sadness. He whispers that he loves me and I
feel my heart squeeze painfully in my chest. I'm trembling
as he sucks on my bottom lip and removes my pants, ca-
ressing my skin as he does. The cotton sheets bunch where
I'm digging my fingers into them as my heart ricochets
against my chest rapidly. He must be able to feel it; I'm all
but waiting for it to burst out of my chest. I fiddle with the
button of his jeans, my intrepidness diminishes and suddenly nerves are getting in the way of my attempt to open
the fastener.

"Here, I got it."

He pushes back on his haunches, flicks the buttons

open and shrugs out of the dark denim. He doesn't take his eyes from me as he grabs his wallet from the pocket, and then tosses the jeans aside and places it on the pillow next to me. His expression has me clamping my thighs trying to ease the stir he's rousing. I watch as the corner of his mouth lifts and his dimples appear from my movement. He's looking at me with such reverence I don't think I'll ever be able to convey in words how this makes me feel.

I'm transfixed on his face and miss the way he removes his underwear. He pulls his shirt up from his back and over his head, breaking the spell, and then he's propped up before me, entirely naked. I greedily scrutinize every inch of his beautiful body. I track the peaks and hollows of his torso, noting the bruising that colors his taught skin. My fingers trace the dips in his abs before moving over his chest. I slow my exploration as it comes to rest over his heart. I can feel the wild thrums vibrate against my palm, and he's looking at me tenderly. I almost smile; thank god he seems to be as nervous as me. I pull him closer with my free arm and place his hand over my heart, so he knows he's not the only one feeling this way. We spend what feels like minutes, but could be hours, silently watching each other and saying so much without uttering a single word. I feel myself sink slightly as the bed slopes and he reaches to pick up his wallet and produces a blue foil square. I use his distraction to remove my shirt and bra. Just do it, I think as I take the packet as he's opening it and gently begin to roll the condom down over him, hypnotized by the moan he lets escape as I push the latex all the way down to his base. I maneuver myself so that he can guide himself into me, and he pulls away furrowing his brow.

"I need to take care of you first, Princess."

I smile at the restraint I know he's trying to exercise and pull him closer.

"I need you inside of me now, Ethan." My voice is embarrassingly breathy and doesn't even sound like my own. Brie would be impressed with the salaciousness of it.

His smile is instant and then I feel him slowly push himself inside of me with careful deliberation. Warmth flows from my head to my toes and I still as every nerve ending ignites and spreads like wildfire through my veins. My toes curl and my heels dig into the mattress.

"Let me know if I hurt you."

I respond by tilting my hips and letting him sink deeper inside. His groan infiltrates my senses and then it's my turn to whimper as he begins rocking into me in a slow deep rhythm. *Nothing has ever felt this good.*

Our bodies collide and become slick with sweat as we move against one another, exulting in the desire and hunger we're trying to sate. I feel as though I'm drowning, and he's my lifeline. I give him all of me, every ounce of passion, every fragment of my heart. He owns me body and soul.

My body thrums as I'm overcome with a surge of intense heat and I'm struck by a rapturous wave of pleasure that rolls over me again and again.

"Blair, I…" His body stills and then I feel him throb inside of me as his shoulders tense and it kick-starts a tirade of aftershocks.

I sink further into the mess of sheets as his body dips and his head drops down to the space between my shoulder and neck.

"Are you okay? Was that okay?"

I smile up at the ceiling and suppress the laugh I want to release.

"It was more than okay, Ethan. In fact, I'm pretty sure it was about perfect."

"Promise?"

This time I do let a laugh escape. "You want me to promise that your bedroom skills are perfect?"

"No." The wetness of his lips skate along my neck before he continues.

"I want you to promise that we are perfect, that what we have is real, and you feel it too; because I haven't allowed anyone or anything into my life for so long, I'm kind of terrified that I'll lose the way I'm feeling right now."

My arms tighten around his waist, and I bow into him, trying to make contact with every inch of his body. I can't seem to get close enough.

"I promise."

elle

He falls asleep, and I spend hours lying tangled within his long limbs, listening to the steady beat of his heart and the little snores that rumble from his chest. I can't turn my thoughts away from the admission he's entrusted me with. My heart physically aches with the gravity of his sadness. How can he think for one moment that his life would be better ended? Tears well up as I imagine him switching off, shutting his body down and standing un-

moving, letting his dad beat him. I have a hard time contemplating what it must have been like for him growing
up. Knowing that the person most little boys look up to as
their hero was responsible for such terrible actions. The
way he told me that he wished his father dead scares me. It
sounded almost sociopathic. Emotionless. Cold. That's not
Ethan; he's funny and witty and has such a beautiful heart.
It tears me apart to think of him in any other way. Maybe
he needs to talk to someone that can help him, a therapist,
or counselor; hell, maybe even a psychiatrist. Someone
that can help him make sense of his emotions regarding
Frank. I don't think I'm the right person for the job. I'm
pretty sure I hate him just as much as Ethan does.

The bed creaks as I untangle myself from Ethan's
legs and slip under his arm. I pick up my cell and pull his
soft cotton Nirvana t-shirt over my head, filling my lungs
with his soapy musky scent. I pad out of the room toward
the bathroom, careful not to trip on the clothes that have
been cast all over the floor in our haste to undress. The
nylon of the carpet tiles scuff on the tips of my toes as I
sneak over to the door. I'm zapped with a bolt of static as I
reach for the handle and cuss under my breath, sneaking a
quick look over my shoulder to make sure I didn't wake
him. I slip around it vigilantly, trying my best not to open
it too far, and expose the light from the street lamp that's
filtering through the tiny window in the corner of the
room. I hold my breath and grit my teeth, as if that would
make some monumental difference as I press the door
closed, hoping I don't disturb him. My stomach lurches as
I press the button on my cell and the home screen illumi-
nates, displaying three new messages from my mom, Brie

and Moira. I scan over the message from my mom, asking for me to let her know how everything is going. I quickly type a reply that lets her know we are both fine and hit the send button before opening Brie's message. I read through the essay-long correspondence that details in impressive depth exactly what she's eaten today, what she will be wearing for her date with Jackson, and how she thinks he could be the one in spite of the fact that this will be their first official date. I smile and make a mental note to respond to her later. Moira's name is highlighted in my list of texts, and I hesitate before opening it. I have to tell her that I can't go along with keeping Ethan in the dark. After the revelations of this evening, and then his words to me after we had made love, I can't risk him finding out that I haven't told him about his mom, especially with all the chances he's given me to tell him. I stare down at the message with my thumb hovering over the screen.

From: Moira
Hi Blair,
How was he after I saw him outside of the restaurant? He seemed unsettled and stressed when I talked to him. He also lied to me about not having remembered anything else. I know you'd said that he only had vague recollections, but I'm worried. Please let me speak to him in my own time. I know what I'm asking of you is hard. Trust me, breaking your son's heart for a second time in a month is harder.

Thank you for keeping me updated. Moira xx

I had envisaged coming in here and sending her a

message, warning her I was going to tell him the truth. Now I'm sitting with my head in my hands on the toilet seat, wishing I'd never agreed to this in the first place. I'm a terrible liar; he's going to notice soon enough and then where does that leave me? I need to fix this; I'm a good person...but apparently a horrible girlfriend.

Chapter 16

Ethan

I'M SCREWED. MY whole body is trembling, my heart feels like a jackhammer slamming excruciatingly into my ribs, and I have no idea what to do with the emotions rotating around in my head. My mind is a giant tumble dryer, and someone's flicked the switch to the spin cycle. I've had my fair share of sex; hell, if I'm honest I've had way more than my fair share, but that wasn't sex. It was two people connecting on a level I've never experienced until now. I mean, sure I've had some really great hook-ups where I've even stayed and had an actual conversation with a chick before leaving, and then at some point found myself going back for more. There was never a connection though. The only driving force behind going back was the assurance that it would be a good time. It's a shallow but truthful fact; sex has always been an outlet, a stress reliever—never anything more, and I've always been happy with that. What Blair and I just did was different, and now

I'm a mess. It was intense but soft; comfortable yet passionate; raw and completely fucking terrifying. I can't help wondering if the first time we did this it felt like that. There's no way, because if it did, I can't even for a second comprehend that I would have forgotten her.

I feel her trying to slide from under my arm; she thinks I'm sleeping—fat chance. I wish I could, but I don't dare. I don't want to wake up later and realize that tonight was just a dream. I wait for the bathroom door to click shut before sitting up and reaching for my cell. The display reads 11:32pm; I thought it would be later than that. My headache from earlier still lingers, it resembles that throbbing feeling you get when you've trapped your hand or foot in a door. After the initial hopping about, screaming shit and cussing like you've just been shot, the pain steadies to a dull, annoying discomfort that won't go away.

"Jeeeesus, Ethan!"

I almost piss my pants at the shriek she lets out as she steps back into the room.

"Sorry," she sighs dramatically, pressing her hand to her chest, the other hanging limp by her side, clutching her cell. "You scared me; I wasn't expecting to walk back into you staring at the door like that. I thought you were sleeping. Damn, my heart feels like it's about to break through my chest."

I watch as she slinks across the floor on her tiptoes, wearing nothing but my t-shirt. It skims the tops of her thighs provocatively and my headache can take a hike; I have no room in my mind right now for anything other than the image of Blair: sleep-tousled, wild crazy sex hair, wearing my clothes. She climbs into bed and I know I'm

111

done; there's no coming back from this now. I may as well hand her my *man card* along with my balls, because she just breezed into the room looking like a goddamn porn star, and all I can think is how much I want to cuddle her. *Kill me now!*

"Are you okay?" she asks as she flips the lamp on. "You look really pale."

"I'm good, Princess." I smile, because really, how am I supposed to answer that? *No, Just give me a moment please. I'm having an internal freak out. The 'me' I thought I knew should be trying to initiate getting back into your pants, but I seem to have grown a vagina and really just want to ask you for a hug!* Yeah, so not happening.

"You look tense—want me to rub your back or shoulders? Mom gets tension headaches, and she swears that a massage helps."

"This is probably the only time I'll ever decline that offer." I grin and pull her onto my lap so she's straddling me.

"My shoulder still aches like a bitch, and I don't think it would be a good idea to massage me there." Her brows shoot up to her hairline as she takes in the suggestive lilt of my voice and the smirk I'm wearing. "You could always massage me somewhere else." I grind my hips upwards and press myself into her, letting her feel what she does to me. "I'm sure you can find another place that really, really needs some rubbing right now."

"Ew! Pervert, I was trying to be nice," she giggles.

"Trust me, it would be better than nice."

"Your incorrigible, Mr. Jamison, and somewhat depraved. I require a little more than a few innuendoes to get my pheromones flowing."

"Hell, baby, I love it when you talk nerdy to me." I wink. I feel her tense in my lap and can't contain my grin. "The wink gets to you, doesn't it?"

"Let me put it to you this way," she says as she drapes her arms around my neck and moves millimeters from my lips. "If I ever see you wink at another girl from this point forward, I think I might go alpha and rip her hair out. The winks are mine."

"Shit, that's hot." I pull her tighter to me and she zeros in on my mouth. I lick my lips waiting for her to kiss me, but she hovers over them, teasingly.

"I feel kind of powerful right now."

My body screams for her to make a move. I'm so turned on I'm a little worried I might blow without her even needing to kiss me.

"I think I like teasing you like this, it's—" I buck my hips, twist and let her fall onto her back before positioning myself over her and pinning her arms above her head with one hand.

"Weren't you ever taught that it's not nice to tease, Princess?" She gasps or groans—or maybe it's a mixture of the two—and it's sexy as fuck. "I think maybe I should teach you a lesson."

"Oh my gosh, that was cheesy!" She beams.

"Yeah, it sounded kinda lame as it came out," I agree. "Is it working though?"

"Yeah, sadly it is. Maybe I have a thing for lame now."

"Nah, Princess, you just have a thing for crazy sexy

musicians."

She groans, and I laugh.

"No I was right the first time, it's the lameness; it's like an aphrodisiac."

"Okay, enough with the lameness. Shut up for a second and let me kiss you."

"Aw, baby…you have such sweet pillow talk. I can't bel—" I silence her as my tongue plunges into her mouth, and then for the next couple of hours I make it my sole mission in life to hear her scream my name.

𝓮𝓵𝓮

Morning rolls around way too quickly for my liking. The shower is making an awful hum and Blair's no longer by my side. I stretch my arms out and relish the aches that are a result of the evening's antics, and not the ones caused by the crash. Can you have good and bad aches? I'm pretty sure I could get used to the ones she causes. I roll onto my side, noticing that her cell is lit up. I don't mean to be nosey but I catch that the screen has my mom's name across it, and I'm instantly at war with myself. I want to see what my mom's texting my girlfriend, but I don't want to do anything that would break Blair's trust. I'm pretty sure reading her text message is recipe for disaster, so against my instincts I turn over and try ignoring it. I'm flirting with the idea of getting dressed when I hear the faint noise of her singing in the shower. My whole body heats as I strain to listen to what it is that she's singing; the din of the shower is muffling it and making it hard to decipher, so I sneak like a complete creeper into the bathroom and lower myself onto the toilet seat while I listen to her sing the chorus of Hinder's, *Better Than Me*. She's good. I guess I shouldn't be surprised, she gives off the vibe that she would be ridiculously talented at anything she tries. I close my eyes listening to her voice and let it wash over me; I've always liked this song. I make a mental note to learn the music and suddenly I'm not here anymore. Instead, I'm sitting in my bathroom at the pool house, watching her brace against the answers to the questions she's asking about my dad and the bruises on my ribs. I blink rapidly, trying to focus the haze of images that play in my mind. I think I remember a party and her being wasted after singing the cup song. I don't know if it's my mind playing tricks or if it's an actual memory. My temples start to ache where I'm pushing my fingers into the pressure points, trying to coax out more of my subconscious but get nothing for my efforts. I'm beyond pissed at this situation now. I just want to be able to remember my life, even if it is a pretty shitty one.

The steam forming in the tiny room is damp on my skin. I figure that as long I'm in here, I should make the most of it and hijack her shower. I pull the curtain back ready for her to shriek at me, but her back is turned while she's soaping up her hair, still singing to herself. I watch as the suds slide down her back and over her ass.

This was definitely one of my better ideas.

I step in behind her, and she starts as I press my front to her back, circling her waist with my arms and telling her to keep singing. I close my eyes and stand holding her as I feel the warmth of the water and the heat of my desire for her douse me.

Chapter 17

Blair

WE ARE TWO hours from home, and I could not be happier. My ass went numb hours ago and I'm starving. The candy I've OD'd on from the last gas station we stopped at must have hyped me up. I'm on a complete sugar rush; I haven't been able to keep still this whole journey. My legs have bopped around so much, I'm sure they'll ache like I've run a marathon tomorrow.

"Are there any Red Vines left?" Ethan asks rummaging around in the bag between us while keeping his focus on the road. It was overflowing with candy and chips a little way back; now, not so much.

"Um…nope, I ate them all. Sorry."

"What, like all of them? There were three packs!"

"Yep, see?" I stick my tongue out like the seven year-old I seem to have reverted to and show him the evidence of my binge. My whole mouth is stained an unnatural cherry red color. "I was hungry."

He regards me with a look of wonderment for a moment.

"Wow, you're kind of a pig."

"Oh my gosh! You can't say that to a girl, you'll give me a complex," I huff in a disgruntled tone; I can't believe he just called me a pig!

"Chill, Winston."

"Huh?" I scrunch my nose not understanding his saying.

"Chill, Winston…it's a quote."

I look at him blankly, and he laughs.

"From that Guy Richie movie. You know…the one where the guy turns up to some drug dealer's loft with a girl that's completely off her ass on weed. He's carrying fertilizer, and one of them shouts at him for not looking like 'your average horti-fucking-culturist'," he says making air quotes. "The dude replies, 'Chill, Winston' in a spaced out voice."

"Yeah, er, no. No clue what film you're referring to," I answer with a skeptical look. "I think you're just making that up."

"What? No way! It's called *Snatch*. No wait, it's the other one, er, *Lock Stock* or something."

"Ooh, *Snatch* is the one with Brad Pitt as a boxer, isn't it?" I must have made a dreamy face because he's looking at me horrified.

"Are you crushing on Brad Pitt?"

"Yeah," I answer wide-eyed. "It's Brad Pitt. Who wouldn't?"

"Seriously? Homeboy's like fifty—that's kinda gross."

"You did not just say homeboy!" I hold my breath trying to contain the laughter.

"You know, you have an uncanny ability to make me feel like a complete douche. No one ever calls me out on what I say, or the way I say it. I normally make this shit sound good. I could make up a goddamn word and everyone at school would be using it inside a week!"

This time my laughter rips through the car like a sonic boom. I clutch at my side and hold my palm over my bandage, trying to ease the discomfort in my stomach that my outburst causes.

"Gretchen, stop trying to make fetch happen! It's not going to happen!"

"What?"

"It's a *Mean Girls'* quote," I say, swiping at a tear my laughter is causing. I can tell I've lost him and he has no clue what I'm talking about. "Sorry, never mind."

"Yeah, I think someone's had way too much candy. I'm cutting you off."

"No way!" I yell trying to grab at the bag he's just snatched from the seat.

"Maybe you're like, hyperglycemic or something..."

"You moron, if I was hyperglycemic I'd be completely strung out and tired."

"Wow. Easy there, tiger, there's no need for the name calling."

I slump back down in my seat with a petulant scowl.

"Okay, well in that case, can we stop there?" I point to an IHOP we're about to pass.

"I don't know. Can I trust you to behave like a normal human if we do?"

I puff my lips and mutter how rude he is under my breath, and he rolls his eyes and pulls into the parking lot.

ele

It turns out that I do actually have a limit to the amount of pancakes I can consume. I'd been determined to prove Ethan wrong and finish the absurdly high stack in front of me, but I've been defeated, and I'm the polar opposite of a gracious loser. If someone placed a pin near me at this very moment, it would only take the slightest prick and I'd burst.

"Told you you'd never finish them," he grins triumphantly as his cocky ass smirk slides into place, the one that's usually reserved for school or when he's performing. He moves his empty plate over to the side and slides my half-full one in front of him.

"Yeah, yeah whatever. No one likes a smart ass," I chime, leaning back in my seat and feeling the undying urge pop the button on my jeans and lay out across the booth.

"I think I'm about to go into a diabetic coma. Seriously, you can't really want to finish mine, too."

"I do, and I will. Your problem, Ms. Thomas, is that you have no stamina," he says dumping more maple syrup on top of the already sugar-coated sticky food.

"I want to argue that," I say pressing my fist into my chest, trying to contain the burp that's bubbling its way up my body. *Please lord, do not let me belch in front of him.* Nothing screams 'she's a keeper' like passing wind in public. "But I'm in no position to do so at the moment, so let's talk about something else, okay?"

"Sure. What do you want to talk about?"

The fizzing in my chest subsides and I breathe a little sigh of relief; the victory is small, but welcomed. I want to broach the subject of our discussion yesterday and ask him to go and see someone, get help, but I have no idea how to do it. He seems in such a good mood at the moment; I'm not sure I want to rock the boat just yet.

"Spit it out, Princess. You obviously want to say something, and it's written all over your face. What's up?"

I swallow and take a deep breath. It's better now than never, right? *Just do it, Blair.*

"I was thinking about what you said to me, you know, about your dad…and the thing is, well, I…" His face has lost its playful edge; his eyes are narrowed and he drops his fork and sits back crossing his arms over his chest. I'm no body language expert, but it's pretty clear that he's pissed I'm mentioning it.

"Okay, I'm just going to say it. I think you should go and see a therapist." I fix myself, ready for an outburst, for him to shout, get mad, annoyed and tell me no way. What I didn't expect was for him to look like I'd just sucker punched him. I watch as the color drains from his face and his shoulders concave as he squirms in his seat, visibly shrinking before me.

"You think I need help?"

I've never heard Ethan's voice sound so weak and exposed, like a child who's just learned that Santa doesn't exist and wants his momma to reassure him that he's wrong. My heart breaks a little as I watch the confidence drain from him. His cockiness and swagger swirl around in an invisible vortex until the essence of what makes him Ethan Jamison—singer, musician, Mr. Popularity—is gone. Like it's been sucked through some imperceptible plughole, leaving a shadow of the guy I know and love sitting before me. Broken.

"I think if you talked to someone it might make you feel better. I don't know, I guess that when Em died I shut down for a little while, and wouldn't talk to my mom about it. She made me an appointment with a grief counselor. Yeah, I only went like three times, but just voicing what was hurting inside helped me in ways I didn't even realize I needed to be helped. I think you should at least explore the possibility."

"It's not that easy…I don't think I can. It's not like I have your regular run-of-the-mill daddy issues, Blair. I don't want to talk about him with a stranger or anyone, for that matter. I definitely don't want to tell them about my fucked up home life. I'm fine. I don't need some overpaid asshole in a leather recliner and plaid button down telling me it's okay to cry. Trying to drag up why it is that he beats me and why the fuck I let him."

"Ethan, I…"

"I need some air," he says balling his napkin and throwing it down on the table along with a few bills to cover the check.

He's out of the exit before I can even process what he's said. I sit in the booth and watch through the window as he steps out into the dirt parking lot and begins kicking at the ground with the toe of his boot. Red dust is swirling around him as he shoves his hands down into the pockets of his jeans, holding his arms rigid and tight by his side. I sigh as he stands and studies the ground like it's the most interesting thing on the planet. I should give him a couple of minutes to himself, but I've never been good at realizing when to take a step back. Knowing what he's told me he thinks about only fuels my need to get to him quicker. I can deal with him wishing Frank dead, but the thought of him wanting his own life cut short scares the shit out of me.

I'm already out of the booth. I step out into the muggy air and make my way over to him. He hasn't moved from his stance. I don't know what to say, so I step up behind him and practically bear hug him. Pushing my face into the back of his shirt. I can feel his breath hitch, but he doesn't say anything. We stand in silence with nothing but the passing traffic humming in the background. Just as I'm about to drop my arms he turns and scoops me off the ground, letting my legs dangle loosely. His arms are so tight around me it feels like my chest has molded into his. I don't think anyone can distinguish where he ends and I begin.

"I'm sorry."

I crane my head back as much as his embrace will allow and look at the sadness he's wearing.

"Why are you apologizing? It's me that needs to say sorry, I should never have brought it up."

"I'm sorry for making you worry about me. I should never have said anything to you."

I wriggle out of his hold, dropping the few inches down to the ground with a thud.

"Yes you should have. I care about you. If you're hurting, or confused or just pissed at life, I want to know about it, Ethan. I don't care how big or small you think it is I want to know every little thing. Don't shut me out. I love you, every part of you, not just the happy-go-lucky, cocky parts but the broken, shattered pieces and everything in between."

My eyes are stinging as I fight back my tears. I can't let them fall, though. I need to be strong for him, show him that I can take the weight of some of his burdens. The tension leaves my shoulders as he leans forward and cups my face, his callused fingers slide from my cheeks and into my hair. Slowly he draws my head to his lips and lands the softest kiss I've ever felt to my forehead.

"Let's go home Princess," he whispers. I take a deep breath, drawing in the smell of his shirt and realize that I am home because I'm with him.

ele

"Are you vibrating?"

"Um, what?" I ask looking perplexed at his question.

"I can hear vibrating—is your cell ringing?"

"Oh!" I rummage in my purse lying open at my feet and fish out my phone, careful not to bend too quickly. It's lit up with Brie's name blinking at me.

"It's Brie. I'm gonna take this," I say putting the phone on speaker.

"Oh my god, you answered!" she squeals. "I've tried calling you a bunch today and it kept going to voicemail."

"Hey, Brie. What's up?"

"I just wanted to know what time you and that sexy ass boy of yours will be getting back. Jackson and I thought we could come and visit with you if it's early enough."

There's hope in her voice and I realize now that I've actually missed her quite a bit. Ethan chuckles faintly at her referring to him as my sexy ass boy, and I smile over at him.

"I don't know…what time are we going to get back, Boy?" I ask and his voice lowers to a husky drawl.

"Ain't no boy here, Princess, I'm all man."

"Oh my god, Blair! Am I on speaker phone?" Brie shrieks as I laugh at the suggestive eyebrow dance he's doing.

"Yeah," I answer as Ethan shouts, "Hi, Brie!"

"Dude, that is not cool! You tell a girl before you put her on speakerphone! Jeez, I could have said anything!"

"When has that ever stopped you before?" I smile.

"Ugh, I'm wounded Blair!" She sighs theatrically. I'm sure if I were standing with her right now, she'd have her wrist to her brow; she has a real flair for the dramatic.

"So, seriously though, can we see you guys tonight or not? If you need time to get sorted, or freakeyyyy," she sings. "We can come by some other time."

I look at Ethan for confirmation and he answers for me.

"We'll be back within the hour. Give me time to drop Blair home with her bags so she can see her mom. Then maybe y'all can come over around eight?"

He looks at me for confirmation and I nod as Brie tells him it's a date and will see us both soon.

"You sure you're up to this?" I ask, once the call has disconnected.

"Yeah, it's only Brie and Jackson. It'll be fine."

"Okay." I smile. He's been quiet and looked pretty down since we left IHOP, maybe seeing a friend will cheer him up a little. I cross my fingers and lean back in my seat, waiting for him to initiate a conversation. He doesn't; instead he looks like he's carrying the weight of the world on his shoulders and my heart squeezes a little bit more.

Ethan

I'VE BEEN RACKING my brain since we were at the restaurant where Blair had mentioned Em's death. The name is familiar to me, and I couldn't place why until I dropped Blair off at her house (which, by the way, I needed directions to. How fucked up is it that I didn't know how to get to my own girl's house?) I carried her things up to her room as she stood hugging her mom in the hall like she hadn't seen her in years. It made me smile; I love that she has that with her mom; I wish I had it with mine. I placed her duffle on her bed and looked around her room. I even sniffed her pillow. I'm a goddamn creeper. That's when I noticed it—the picture on her noticeboard. It was of me at my locker and Em standing to the side, but still in the forefront of the picture. It was strange, like she was supposed to be the focal point but instead I was. I walked over to get a closer look, and that's when I was flat out assaulted with the images of Blair crying while I shouted at her about being part of Emily's bucket list. I needed to spend a few minutes trying to jumble through the mixed-up memories, but they were there. We'd argued about her crossing me off as a checkbox on her dead best friend's list. I'd left her at the campsite where we'd collected our shit yesterday, and went and got trashed at a dive bar.

I know I'm still missing some vital points to complete the picture, but I don't want to ask Blair to fill them in for me. I'm pretty sure that we got past the argument, but I have a weird feeling that I'm still pissed at her. I just don't remember why. Maybe it's because it feels new again and I need a while to get my head around it. Perhaps it's just my newfound insecurity but she regarded me with such a strange look when I finally returned downstairs, I'm finding it hard to stay confident when I know I'm still partially in the dark.

I made small talk with Susan for a few minutes and assured her that I would go and collect my medication and check in with the hospital in the morning. Blair followed me out to my car and gave me a kiss, declaring she'd be coming over to my place at eight before I headed home.

That's where I am now. My feet are resting on the walnut coffee table in the family room, boots still on, and my bags are dumped on the sofa next to me. I'm waiting for the asshole to walk in and kick off at what I'm doing, even though I know he isn't here. My headache is back, but I think this one is because I can't stop my brain from trying to figure out the missing pieces to my memory of the accident. I've reasoned that my dad came to the police station and bailed Blair and me out. I'm pretty sure that's a memory and not just my overactive imagination playing tricks on me. What I can't figure out is how the crash happened, or at least what happened between the time we left the cop shop and waking up in the ICU.

Dad stands mocking me from the family portrait that hangs above the fire; it was taken when I was about twelve years old. I'm sitting in the middle of the frame; Mom is standing behind me to my left, Dad to the right, and they both have one of their hands resting on my shoulders. Anyone looking at the picture would see nothing untoward about it, but if you look closely you can tell my smile's pained. I remember right before it was taken my parents were arguing because Dad had arrived home late. Mom had cooked his dinner and it was ready for him to eat, after which he was going to change and we'd make our way downtown to the portrait studio. Dad had just changed out of his uniform and into his tailored navy blue suit. He was walking through the kitchen to the island with his plate in hand, and I'd run downstairs with my head down playing on my PSP. I didn't see him—it was just an accident. The plate fell and covered his suit pants in food before smashing on the tiled floor.

I can still recall the second just before his fist connected with my stomach…it was slowed down, like god wanted to let me get a good look at the hate on his face as his first travelled towards me. I remember having enough time to think that it was better to try and not tense. I knew from experience it hurt less that way, but I was a twelve-year-old kid with a man's fist sailing towards him. Of course, I tensed. I practically shit my pants. He hit me so hard that I flew across the room and threw up where I landed. Then he walked past me like nothing had happened and went and got changed. Mom cleaned me up, not saying anything worth remembering. An hour later we were all smiling for the camera. I fucking hate that picture.

ele

Blair arrives before the others. She smiles, following me into the family room before noticing the glass shattered all over the mantle and in front of the fire. The portrait frame is smashed and resting in the corner.

"What happened?" she asks quietly.

"Not sure. I guess it must have fallen from the wall while we were away." The lie falls from my lips effortlessly, like they always do. I'm practiced at it. *How did you get that bruise?* Playing basketball. *What happened to your shoulder?* Walked into the doorframe drunk. They're second nature now.

She looks around the room before turning to face me.

"What happened?" she asks again in a sterner voice, knowing I'm lying. I figure I should just tell her the truth.

"I hate that picture. I decided to do something about it." I shrug and glance over at the fire poker I smashed into the portrait minutes before she arrived. Her gaze follows mine and a frown pulls at her lips.

"Go grab a trash bag and the vacuum cleaner; let's get rid of the glass."

"You don't have—"

"Ethan," she sighs and I nod.

"Okay, gimme a second."

I return with a garden bag and the vacuum. I place the large shards inside the bag along with the broken frame and the picture, as Blair hoovers up all the smaller pieces.

"I never liked this photograph of you anyway," she says, looking at a corner of it sticking out from the sack. "Your smile's fake."

I shoot her a real smile. Everyone always commented on what a beautiful family picture it was.

"I love you."

"I love you, too," she says like it's no big deal, wrapping the power cord up and securing it back in place. She has no idea how comforting it is to hear her say it, like it's the most natural thing in the world.

The sound of laughter filters into the room seconds before the doorbell chimes.

"You get that. It's most likely Brie and Jackson. I'll get rid of this," she says picking up the bag and disappearing out of sight.

"Well, if it ain't Evel Knievel," Jackson says, his 6-foot, solid frame pushing through the door and giving me a bro hug. It hurts but I don't complain.

"Who?" Brie asks stumbling behind as TJ tries to push through. Her long blonde hair falls over her face in a veil and she tosses it back like she's starring in some shampoo commercial.

"Dude, your girlfriend, doesn't know who Evel Knievel is!" TJ laughs, giving me the same bro hug Jackson just did and nearly collapses my lungs when he slaps my back. I wince and groan as he sucks air in through his teeth and offers me an apologetic smile that's more of a grimace.

"Girlfriend?" I look to Jackson who's wearing a shit-eating grin.

"Yep," Brie giggles, twisting a piece of her hair around her finger. "Good to see you, Ethan," she says kissing my cheek.

"Woah…back away from my boy toy!" Blair shouts, and then Casey appears from nowhere, pushing past me at the same time Brie does to tackle Blair to the wall and hug her. She smiles awkwardly and I find it completely fucking adorable.

"Boy Toy!" Drew sniggers, filing in with Dannii in tow. "Glad to see you, man."

"Yeah, you too." I take the sight of them in for a moment: he's wearing jeans and a tight plain black t-shirt with a black leather jacket. She's wearing the same, just a tighter version.

"You had us all real worried. Dipshit over there would have had to take your place as lead." I smile as TJ turns and flips Drew the bird.

"Are they coordinating their clothes or something?" I ask TJ under my breath as we file into the kitchen and grab drinks.

"Yep," he sniggers as he pushes Drew's back, "She's pussy whipped him good!" he barks out.

"Screw you!" Drew retorts uninterestedly, not bothering to even turn. Dannii does though, and if looks could kill, TJ would be so dead they'd have to bury him twice.

We sit around the island talking. Blair handles most of the questions, seeing as how I can't really recall shit, and I sit back, happy to let her do it as she perches on my lap.

"You know you look like shit, right?" Jackson tells me before taking a long pull on his beer. Everyone is in the kitchen, laughing and joking. I'd slipped out to clear my head, and Jackson followed. I fiddle with an invisible piece of lint on my leg as I look out over the pool.

"Thanks, man."

"Seriously, bro, you okay? I heard what's going on with your old man. Your mom called my mom. You know how they are…she said he needed a pretty big op."

"I don't really want to talk about it, but thanks."

"Hey, no pressure…if you do though, I'm here."

We stare at each other for a beat too long and it's weird as hell.

"Dude, should we like hug or shit?" he says, and I push him off the side of the lounger he's settled on.

"Quit being a pussy."

"Score! Who's pussy are we talking about?" TJ asks with a grin as he takes a seat.

"Your mom's!" Jackson and I deadpan in unison.

"That's gross, assholes! So, you guys do realize I'm the only single one now since this dick," he points to Jackson who scowls in return, "decided to shack up with the rack on legs inside."

"Dude that's my fucking girlfriend—don't call her that!"

"Seriously, YOU were calling her that a few days ago!"

I laugh and look over at Jackson. "How did that come about? Since when do you do girlfriends?"

"Says Mr. Bang Them and Bail himself! Things

change; you of all people should get that. I like her, she's cool."

I nod knowingly and TJ groans.

"What the hell is up with everyone? Damn, next you'll be braiding each other's hair and talking about your periods syncing and shit." Jackson and I laugh as he stares at us disappointedly. "I'm going back inside. Casey talks better smack than you two powder puffs." With that, he steals Jackson's beer and disappears into the house hollering for someone to turn the chick music off.

Jackson leans forward and blows out a breath. "So I need to give you a heads up; there are some rumors circulating around school. I'm not sure if you and Blair are planning on being there Monday morning, but I thought you should know."

"Okay, what rumors?" I ask feeling suddenly on edge.

He cringes a little before answering through gritted teeth. "That you were hooking up with Della before you and Blair set off on your trip. You didn't, did you?"

I stare at him with a panicked look on my face.

"Shit. You did, didn't you?"

"What? No! At least, I don't think I did. Fuck, I don't know…I have amnesia for god's sake! I wouldn't do that to her. I love her, I…I…" My leg thrusts out as I kick the lounge chair TJ just vacated in a fit of frustration, and watch as it digs into the lawn and tumbles onto its side.

"It sounds like something I would have done before Blair. What if I did?"

"What if you did what?" she asks, appearing on the patio.

Fuck.

"Um, I'll be inside," Jackson says, giving me a wide-eyed stare that tells me I'm screwed as he passes.

I run my hands over my head and grip the back of my neck. She stays unmoving, like she knows I'm about to say something she doesn't like. I pull her into my lap and kiss her temple quickly. "Don't be mad okay?"

"That's the worst opener to a conversation you could ever say, Ethan!"

I take a deep breath and tell her about the rumors in one long exhale.

"Did you do it?"

"Truthfully? I don't know; I don't remember. But I swear to you, Princess, the way I feel about you…I don't think I could have. I love you, Blair, honestly. I can—" my flustered rambling is cut off as she places two fingers over my mouth, silencing me.

"Della's jealous. She pretty much hates me, and I wouldn't be surprised if she's started these stories up herself to break us up. If you say you think you didn't do it, then I believe you."

My jaw goes slack, and I look at her in awe. "As easy as that?" I say in a disbelieving tone and watch the frown grip her lips.

"Yeah, I trust you Ethan. One hundred percent."

I kiss the frown right off her beautiful face until her lips are swollen and my chest burns from the lack of oxygen. I'm about to delve in for more when her cell starts to beep.

"It's probably my mom messaging me," she says retrieving the phone from her back pocket. The screen says, 'Moira' and I glower, remembering it's not the first time

I've noticed my mom texting her. Blair's eyes dart to mine and then to her cell, and I get an uneasy feeling in the pit of my stomach.

"Why's my mom been texting you?"

She stays quiet a beat too long and my anxiety grows.

"I'll explain when everyone has gone home, okay?" The way she answers doesn't overly inspire my confidence that it's nothing to worry about. I slide her off my lap and walk straight into the house, announcing that everyone needs to go because I'm wiped out. Blair looks like she's about to throw up as I close the door after Casey and Brie take a ridiculously long time to say goodbye.

I lean my back against the door, take a deep breath and steel myself for the blow that I'm certain she's about to deliver.

"Okay, Blair. What's going on?"

Chapter 19

Blair

CASEY AND BRIE ambush me as the guys pile into Ethan's front hall. With the exception of how I am with him, I'm most definitely not what you would deem a touchy girly girl. Their assault on me takes me by surprise. They hug me like Em would have, and although I feel awkward I'm also a little taken back at how good it feels to have girlfriends. I miss Em every day; knowing that these two have my back is like a balm soothing the void losing her has caused.

They start talking at a million miles an hour over one another, and my head spins as it whips from side to side. I have no clue who to answer or which one to give my attention to. The decision is made for me when I watch Dannii walk in, hand in hand with Drew. I have barely spoken with her since the day I heard her in the bathrooms at school.

"Blair, so good to see you," she says in her sugary-sweet drawl as she passes by. I'd believe she was being genuine if I didn't know any different. I smile a toothy fake grin that matches her own and lead the way through to the kitchen.

The evening is pretty much spent answering questions about how Ethan and I are doing post-accident. I can't help but take note of the way Dannii sits glaring at me. I need to confront her at some point but tonight is definitely not the night. I have a feeling I'll need my mental strength to be on point, and at the moment I'm totally drained.

I decide to leave the kitchen when Casey and Brie begin to discuss how completely perfect Jackson's body is in an impressively remarkable amount of graphic detail. I blush and feel like I've just seen naked pictures of him. It's so wrong; I shake the mental images from my head and bolt for the backyard when they expect a rundown as to how Ethan's form compares.

I step out onto the patio and find the guys sitting on the loungers. Jackson is leaning forward gritting his teeth while Ethan looks like he's about to have a panic attack. I catch the tail end of their conversation and make my presence known as I join in.

I wasn't expecting to be hit with rumors about him and Della. I watch the worry etch itself firmly onto his features while he stammers that he can't confirm for certain that they're not true. Pre-accident, this would have been an issue. I'd have undoubtedly been crushed, but as I'm looking at him now, I realize that I know the stories aren't true. We spent every day together before we took our trip, and I don't for a second believe that he could act the way he does around me while cheating on me with her. Maybe I'm

ELLE BROOKS

delusional, and this will come back and bite me in the ass, but then again, maybe it won't. If nearly losing Ethan taught me anything, it's that life is too short to worry about the past, and to be grateful that we are lucky enough to have a present.

We're in the middle of a pretty intense make-out session when I stupidly pull my beeping phone from my pocket. Moira's name is flashing like a neon sign and Ethan's already noticed. I want to make an excuse and spare him the pain I'm about to cause, because I know he's going to ask why she's texting me and I'm done with the secrets.

elle

"You lied to me!" It's a statement, not a question, and I wrap my arms tightly around my waist as armor. My heart begins its slow descent into my stomach in response to the look he's pinning on me.

"I didn't lie, Ethan. I just didn't tell you everything. There's a difference, baby."

"That's bullshit and you know it!"

"I swear, I—"

"Shut up, please just shut up for one second. I need to process this."

His links his hands behind his head and paces back and forth while I stand wallowing in my own guilt. I want to cry so badly that it hurts, and I let my head fall backward and blink rapidly, hoping to stop the tears.

"I asked you outside the hospital that day. I fucking asked you, and you promised I could trust you! Have you

138

forgotten that promise?"

"You *can* trust me! I'm telling you now. All I did was agree to give your mom a heads up on how you are, and if you'd remembered anything. I'm telling you this now because I felt uncomfortable with it."

"No, you're telling me this now because I called you out and asked!"

"Ethan, I swear that's not the case. You can check my phone if you don't believe me. I told your mom that I was going to tell you, and she's been blowing up my messages ever since. You just asked before I had a chance to explain things to you."

I knew this was going to happen; I'm an idiot for agreeing to Moira's requests in the first place.

"I'm going to ask this one time Blair, so please don't lie to me. What is it that my mom is worried I'm going to find out about?"

This is it, the moment I've been dreading since Ethan woke up in that hospital bed and didn't know who I was. How am I supposed to tell him that Moira isn't his mom?

"Okay, Ethan, the doctors and your mom really won't be happy if I tell you this. They warned me about causing you too much stress."

"Too much stress? IS THAT A JOKE!" he screams in my face, and I step back stunned. My breath stutters, and I'm trembling. I know he'd never hurt me, but I'd be lying if I said that he didn't just scare the crap out of me. He looks instantly sorry, no doubt because of my reaction.

He throws himself down onto the sofa looking utterly defeated. His head falls into his hands, and I can tell he's trying to control his breathing. I watch silently from where

I'm standing by the fireplace. I have a million emotions running through me, and I don't know what to do. I want to comfort him, but at the same time I'm pissed at his explosive actions. He has every right to be frustrated, but the way he yelled at me is not okay. I slowly make my way across the room and take a seat next to him. He turns his head but stays in the same position and the hurt in his eyes engulfs me.

"I'm sorry," he mouths. I'm not even sure if he makes any sound, the blood rushing through my ears is the only noise I can focus on.

"Please don't make me tell you this. If you wait, it's probably going to come back to you, baby." It was a request, but my voice shakes, and it comes out as more of a plea.

He shakes his head and rubs his hands down his face before sitting up and facing me straight on. "Please, Princess."

I'd justified my actions by telling myself that I wasn't actually doing anything wrong, and if Ethan asked me directly about his mom, I would tell him. The justification was an easy pill to swallow, because I didn't wholeheartedly think I'd have to do it. As naive as it seems now, I thought he'd remember this on his own and I'd be off the hook, or at the very least, Moira would do it. Maybe if I prompt him, his memory will kick in and do my dirty work for me.

"Do you remember anything about *us* before the accident?"

"Yeah, small things. Nothing makes a whole lot of sense though," he replies.

"Okay, so do you remember meeting me at the cinema, and we took a drive down to the beach because you wanted to talk to me?"

The concentration on his face is admirable; I can tell he's racking his brain trying to summon the memory. Sadly, I can also tell when he comes up short. I sigh and reluctantly carry on.

"You came to meet me that day because your mom had just given you some pretty big news, Ethan. We sat at the beach for hours and talked through it."

"Blair, just tell me."

"God, I wish I wasn't the one doing this to you. Okay, the reason you came to meet me and talk that day…was because your mom had told you that she wasn't…" I wipe my palms across my jeans and look away. I don't want to see the effects of the words I'm about to utter. "She told you she wasn't your mom."

Silence.

I've always enjoyed it until now. The tension in the room is unbearable as I wait for him to respond, but he doesn't. We sit quietly for minutes that feel like hours. I can't take it. I think I'd prefer it if he were shouting at me.

"I think you should leave."

My head snaps up from the floor and I look at him. His face is completely devoid of any emotion, and it's scary as hell.

"What?"

"You heard me, Blair. I need to be alone. I'll call you later," he says walking over to the family room door and holding it open.

My heart sinks and my stomach rolls as I stand.

ELLE BROOKS

"Ethan, I—"
"Don't. Okay, just don't. I'll call you later."

I feel the heat of my tears ready to erupt as I brush past him and make my way to the front porch. The door is closed behind me before I have another chance to change his mind.

ele

The smell of hot cocoa permeates the house as I close the back door behind me and move into the kitchen.

"Oh, honey you scared me," Mom says as she turns and finishes making her drink. I don't want to speak. I know that the second I do she'll hear the scratchiness in my voice and demand that I tell her what's wrong.

"I'm making cocoa, would you like…" Her words stick as she looks up and gets a closer look at my tear-stained puffy face.

"Oh, sweetheart, what's wrong?" she asks, moving the pan from the stove and rushing around the island to envelope me in a warm hug.

"I told him about his mom."

I don't need to say anything else; it's blatantly obvious by my presence that it didn't go well. Mom strokes my hair and makes soothing shushing noises as I cry into her shoulder. I know I have only myself to blame, but I'm too tired to not indulge in the pity party I'm currently throwing myself.

"Here," she says leading me to take a seat. "Nothing cheers a person more than chocolate." She walks over to the counter and pours two mugs of cocoa before reaching into the cupboard and pulling out jars and packets.

"Ah-ha," she says, retrieving a bottle of Irish Crème Liquor and adding two big slugs to the drinks. She looks up as she pours and fixes me with a stare.

"I better not catch you doing this when I'm not here," she motions to the alcohol. "You'll be in trouble, understand?"

I give her a weak smile and nod.

"Good. Now, do we go for oatmeal and raisin?" she asks, pulling a pack of cookies from the cupboard and placing them down on the counter. "Or double chocolate chip?"

"Bring on the double chocolate chip. You just said chocolate makes everything better, right?"

She gives a little huff as she walks over and places a mug in front of me along with the full pack of cookies. "It's a temporary fix, but let's worry about that later."

Chapter 20

Ethan

THE SOFT STRAINS of music fill the small room and begin to settle my anxiety, just like it always does. Sitting at my piano has constantly been an escape for me. From the moment my mom began to teach me at the age of four, I've loved it. I don't need to think about anything other than the music—how long the next note is, what rhythm it requires, and how loud to play it. There's no space for the monsters that lurk at the back of my mind once my fingers touch the keys of the Steinway. My concentration isn't focused on not annoying my dad, or worrying that I'm failing at this and that, or not doing well enough in some other area, because I know I can play. It comes naturally, and thankfully, it's probably the only aspect of my life my dad hasn't tainted and ruined.

My fingers stretch over the ivories as I play Debussy's *Clair de Lune*. Pain shoots through my wrist as my hands travel from key to key, but I don't care. I've sat down to this piano in far worse physical states, but I always play consistently. It's one of the first songs that showcased how well I could perform. Mom cried the first time I made it through the entire piece without a mistake. She'd told me that I was born to do this. It's the one memory I have of her that I actually cherish. I bring the piece to its end and rest my head on my arms against the cold wood. It takes seconds for the blanket the music has provided to slip away and leave me feeling cold and exposed. My mom's little secret creeps back into my head, and the vision of Blair breaking it to me makes its way to the forefront of my mind.

How could she? Why didn't she tell me sooner?

I can't take any more. I push away from the piano and slam every door I walk through until I'm out in the back yard. I take a deep breath, willing the crisp air to clear the mess and destruction that Mom and Blair have created in my brain. I stare out at the pool house and suddenly I'm overcome with memories of Blair and me in there, watching movies. I'm not sure what triggered them, but they put me on my ass. I don't know which way is up when I think about her now. I love her so much, but I can't understand how she could know something as important as my mom's admissions and not tell me. Surely, if she felt even half of what I feel for her, she'd have said something sooner.

I stomp back into the house and go straight to the medicine cabinet. I grab the first pack of painkillers I can find and swallow two without water. The chalkiness sticks to my throat as I try and force them down, leaving a horrible taste in my mouth. There's a half-full bottle of beer that one of the guys has left open on the island. I reach over and take a long pull to get rid of the artificial taste filling my mouth. I need this pain to stop. I'm not even sure if it's a headache or heartache anymore. All I know is that I hate it.

ele

More things to chalk up as dipshit things to do:

#1 Take painkillers that aren't prescribed to you.

#2 Wash them down with alcohol.

#3 Scroll through pictures of your hot girlfriend when mad at her. Then drink more to try and wash away the hurt.

#4 Trash your room in a drunken rage.

#5 Leave no water by the bed when you know you're gonna wake up with a hangover from hell and your mouth tasting like ass.

I feel like crap, I look like crap, and according to the alarm that's upside down in the middle of the floor amidst the war zone that is now my bedroom, it's 2:10 pm. I have five minutes to get to my appointment, collect my meds and check in with the doctors.
CRAP!
I leave the house looking like a homeless person. I've brushed my teeth and changed my clothes, and that's about

it. I was obviously still drunk when I did, because I thought I looked okay until some kid in the reception area of the doctor's office told me I'd put my shirt on inside out. Getting schooled by a six-year-old about how to dress was not the highlight of my day. Neither was Dr. Hardy's reaction when she smelled the alcohol on my breath, and then found out I'd been taking my dad's Codeine pills to try stop my headaches. There was a point when I thought that maybe she wouldn't let me leave again. She looked a lot less than happy with me.

After scheduling my physiotherapy appointments for my wrist and booking in to see the brain doc, I'm on my way over to Jackson's. I'm driving in silence, since my head still feels like it's in a damn vice, when my mom's call comes through. I fully intended to ignore it until the pent-up anger surfaced and it was all I could do to pull over and not hit answer and immediately start shouting at her.

"Yeah?" I know it's not the politest way to answer a call, but she's lucky I'm not answering with a string of cusses.

"Oh, thank heavens! I've been calling the house all morning and your cell has been diverting me straight to your voice mail."

"What do you want, Mom?"

"To know how you are. Susan called me this morning and told me that Blair had gone home last night in tears after telling you about me." Her voice is quiet, like she's whispering.

"Where are you, what's with the hushed tone?"

"You know where I am—at the hospital. I've just left

your dad's room; I didn't want him hearing our conversation."

I'm not sure why, but her words seem to be exactly the wrong ones at the wrong time. "Who gives a shit if he hears you! It should be me that you're worried about, not that asshole hearing you tell me that I'm not your goddamn son! Jeez, you're unbelievable."

"Calm down, Ethan. Let me explain. Please?"

"What can you possibly have to explain? Don't you think you've done enough? No, wait, that's wrong. You haven't done enough. You have never done enough when it comes to me!" The venom behind my words is all too evident, and I hear her gasp at my outburst.

"I'm coming home," she tells me. "We need to talk and not over the phone. I'll catch a flight later today."

"Do whatever the hell you want, Moira!" I know I'm an ass when I call her by her name, but I don't care. I want her to hurt. She deserves to feel as shitty as I do.

ele

I pop a few of the prescription pills I collected from the pharmacy and pour myself a huge glass of water. I drove around in a hate-fueled daze for a while after hanging up on my mom. I must have been on autopilot because I ended up back home, only I have no real idea of what route I took to get here. The message on the back of the pill carton said not to operate heavy machinery, and that the pills might make me drowsy. I don't want to be trapped in my own warped headspace, so I decide to call Jackson to come hang out. I normally like my own company, but today, not so much. It takes fifteen minutes before he's waltzing through the door announcing that we should get some practice in. Apparently Kickstart has been booked to play some club in town after graduation. I groan at the thought.

"Dude, you look like I just ran over your dog. What's wrong?"

"I don't have a dog."

"It's just a saying, jackass. Seriously though, what's up?"

"Honestly bro, you don't even want to know."

He drops down into the seat next to me and places his guitar at his feet. He sits back and removes his cap, ruffling up his already messy blond hair and sighs. "Take it Blair didn't react well to the rumor news huh?"

I let out a small laugh. "If only that were it." I drain the glass of water in one long gulp and wipe my mouth on the back of my hand. "She told me that my mom's not actually my mom." I watch as the confusion slides across his face, and his eyes squint.

"What do you mean she's not your mom?"

"Exactly how it sounds, man. Mother Dearest isn't my biological mom."

He rubs the back of his neck, still looking utterly baffled.

"How does Blair know this?"

I let out a huff and rub my temples. "You're asking the wrong amnesia patient. I have no freaking clue what's going on. Only that my mom must have told me at some point before the crash. I must've told Blair, then all the shit with the accident happened. My mom figured since my slate is wiped clean, she just wouldn't tell me again, and enlisted Blair to help her."

People that say that talking through your problems helps, a problem shared is a problem halved and all that rubbish. I call that bullshit; a problem shared is a problem doubled. Jackson sits slack-jawed with an entirely vacant stare. Telling him hasn't made me feel better in the slightest. Now I just feel sorry that I've caused the unease that's descended on the room.

"Dude...fuck!"

"Your words of wisdom are truly inspiring. You know, if college doesn't work out, you could get a gig as a motivational speaker." I'm trying to add humor to the situation. It's not working.

"Sorry, I just don't know what to say. Have you confronted your mom or dad?"

"Mom's flying back today. She wants to talk."

He hisses air through his teeth and gives me a pity glare.

"This really sucks, Ethan. I'm sorry."

"Hey, what's one more thing to deal with, right? Amnesia, a paralyzed father at death's door, a lying girlfriend, and a fake mom. All I need now is a long lost sibling somewhere that I've unsuspectingly slept with, and I can go on Jerry Springer."

His mouth lifts at the corner as he suppresses his amusement.

"Gross."

"It would be just my luck right now."

"So, what happened with Blair? Are you guys okay? Still speaking? Dating?"

"I dunno, Jackson."

I drop my head into my hands and begin massaging my temples with my fingers again. *Why won't this headache let up?*

"I kind of kicked her out, as soon as she told me."

"You didn't make her explain?" he asks, disbelieving. I cringe a little and shake my head no. The movement makes me dizzy. The pills seem to be kicking in, and I feel tired.

"I couldn't take anymore lies."

"How do you know she would lie to you?"

His voice sounds like an echo from really far away. I squeeze my eyes a couple of time to fight the weird lights buzzing in my peripheral vision. Then I watch his face appear in front of mine. His mouth's moving, but it's in slow motion and there are no words coming out.

I frown.

Blink.

My eyes are heavy.

Darkness.

Chapter 21

Blair

"HE'S GOING TO be pissed when he comes around and realizes that I'm here." I run my hand through Ethan's hair, and pull the blanket a little higher over his lax position on the couch.

"Don't worry, I'll take the heat. I didn't know who else to call," Jackson says rubbing his neck and stretching.

"Um…the ambulance?" I deadpan.

"Yeah, and we both know he'd have taken that real well! He only took three pills from what I could get out of him before he passed out completely," he says rattling the packet millimeters from my face.

"The directions say that they'll make you drowsy. He just needs to sleep them off."

"Okay, are you sure he only took three?"

He sighs and opens the little white box showing me that there are only three missing from the foil blister packet.

"I guess we should just wait then."

"Yup," he answers with a hint off sass behind the word.

"Jackson, have I done something to make you pissed? What's with the attitude?"

He looks at me like I'm an idiot, and I'm even more confused.

"He told me," he says with a glare. I raise my palms, jut my head out and widen my eyes, indicating that I'm still no wiser.

"About you lying to him about his mom!"

And there's the clarity I needed. My shoulders drop, and I remove my glasses before rubbing at the bridge of my nose and replacing them. Jackson is watching me intently, no doubt waiting for me to defend my actions.

"You don't know all of it. So please don't judge me."

"He's totally cut up. I know that much."

"I know."

"You need to fix this, Blair. I've never seen him so happy as when he's with you. You have to make things right."

If he only knew how much I wish that I could. I'd do anything to take away his pain.

"I'll try," I lament, brushing past him to refill Ethan's glass for when he wakes. Jackson reaches out and takes a hold of the top of my arm, halting me in my tracks. I jerk backward and glare at his hand gripping me.

"Not good enough. Don't just try; make it happen."

I nod and pull myself free. I don't know what I'm going to say to him when he wakes. But I'm not leaving so easily this time.

"Look, I hate to do this," Jackson says. "I kind of need to leave. I'm supposed to be picking Brie up in half an hour from her cheer practice. Are you okay to stay with him?"

"Of course I am. I'm not just going to bail on him." I respond with a little more despondency than intended. He checks his watch then looks down at his cell.

"I can call her and ask if she can catch a ride with someone else," he says looking over at Ethan then back to his cell.

"No, honestly, I'll be fine. We need to talk anyway. I won't leave him on his own if that's what you're worried about. I'm not a heartless bitch."

"I know you're not, Blair." He gives me a sad smile and walks over to the door. His massive frame lingers before he finally turns.

"Tell him to call me if he needs anything. His mom should be back tonight, although he didn't say when."

I feel my eyes bug out a little. "Later."

"Yeah, later."

Moira's coming back? I'm not sure how I feel about that little nugget of information. On one hand, I'm glad she's finally putting his needs first and decided to come deal with this mess. On the other, I'm pissed at her for not telling him sooner. I get what she was trying to do; I guess I'm just mad at myself for not changing her mind.

elle

His legs kick out as he bolts upright with a start. I feel my heart jump into my throat and watch in slow motion as my coffee soars through the air, floating like a lead balloon before dousing us both in the lukewarm liquid. I let out a startled screech as Ethan dives from the sofa, pulling his shirt over his head in one fluid movement. It's so fast the coffee couldn't have even had time to soak through to his skin. He lunges forward and yanks my t-shirt over my head, painfully pulling half my hair with it.

"The fuck! Ouch, you've got a hold of half my scalp! Get off!" I cry out.

"Shit, sorry. Are you burned?" he says in a panic, alarm and confusion evident in his eyes.

"No, I've been drinking it for the last half hour. It's barely even warm."

He lets out a relieved grunt. "Why'd you decide to throw coffee over us?"

"I didn't!" I shriek. The shock of the last thirty seconds has my voice reaching heights I'm sure only dogs can register. He gives me a look of complete perplexity. "Okay, so I'm imagining the fact that we're both standing here half-naked and covered in coffee, then?"

"Don't be a smart ass. You were sleeping. I was sitting next to you on the sofa, drinking my coffee. You must have been dreaming, because one minute you were all serene and calm, and the next you jumped up like someone was attacking you. You knocked my drink out of my hands."

He looks around, as if only now realizing his whereabouts.

"Are you okay?" I ask. He's as pale as a ghost.

"Yeah." He takes a few calming gulps of air. "I was just frightened you might be scalded is all. I didn't mean to drag your shirt off like that," he says with a hint of amusement in his tone. His eyes drop from mine down to my chest then back up, before repeating the cycle again. And again, and again. Men!

I glance down at my chest for a second before I realize that I'm staring at my boobs, and not my bra. What the hell?

My arms fly up to cover myself. I can feel the heat spreading through my cheeks like wildfire, and know I must be glowing bright red. My embarrassment only flames his amusement and now he's flat-out laughing at me. There's not a hint of remorse as he looks down at my shirt in his hand and then fishes out my sports bra from the soggy crumpled fabric and tosses it at me.

What do I do? The same as anyone would do when someone throws something at you—try to catch it. Except I've momentarily forgotten why my hands were indisposed. I reach out to intercept my bra and feel the weight of my breast shift slightly. I miss the bra, and it hits me in the face and falls at my feet as I retract my hands at warp speed, trying to protect my modesty, or at least what's left of it. Ethan's whole face contorts.

Asshole.

"Holy shit! That worked out better than expected," he says through his laughter. He's clutching his sides and his shoulders are bobbing up and down as he fights a losing battle to gain control. As much as I want to be annoyed at him, it is kind of funny— in an undignified, and horribly embarrassing kind of way.

"This doesn't mean that I'm not still mad at you, but the peep show just cheered me up," he smirks. "Follow me, Princess," he requests and I oblige, too dumbstruck to do anything other than tail behind, trying to pull the sports bra over my head with one arm.

He takes me up to his room and I'm wondering what his intentions are, given that he not-so-subtly dropped in that I'm still not his favorite person. He opens his dresser and retrieves a faded Stones t-shirt, shaking it out and looking from me to the shirt and then deciding that it won't do. He rummages around and pulls out a plain white t-shirt, inspects it and then seems satisfied. He walks over to me, crossing the room in a few long strides and stands millimeters from me.

"Arms."

"Huh?"

"Arms," he says again smiling while I stand there fighting the urge to pounce on him. He looks good enough to eat. His hair's tussled from sleep, and he's barefoot and wearing a pair of low-slung jeans, his boxers peeping out just above the waistband. His chest still bears the yellowing bruises from the crash, but they don't detract from the tanned smooth skin stretched over the peaks and dips of his abs. I could stand here and stare at his torso all day without tiring.

"Lift your arms, babe!"

"Oh, right…yeah. Sorry."

He pulls the t-shirt over my head and then looks down at my jeans. They look like a poorly executed Jackson Pollock imitation; dirty, soggy, dark splat marks cover a good proportion of blue.

"Take them off; I'll put them in the wash."

I hesitate for a second but figure that if he washes my

clothes it will give me at least an hour to try and reason with him before he can throw me out. I mean, heck, he wouldn't toss me outside without any clothes...*hopefully.*

"Okay," I tell him, peeling the damp material down my legs. I look up and catch his eyes watching me. I figure now's as good a time as any to talk.

"Ethan, I wanted to—"

"Not now." He holds his palms up and cuts me off immediately, obviously knowing where I was intending to take the conversation.

"Fine, here."

I let the denim drop to my feet, and then kick my jeans up at him. He catches them with a crooked grin before disappearing out of the room again.

I walk around his bedroom looking at the knick-knacks spread out over his dresser. I take a guitar pick and move it between my fingers before setting it back down. I pick up a ratty old notebook and flip to where the page marker is. It's music. Like real notes, not just letters and words. I smile, a weird sense of pride swelling in my heart. Then I notice the title: *Rescued By a Princess*, and I can't help but wonder if he's referring to me.

I look down at myself, and decide that his t-shirt is just about long enough to get away with wearing downstairs since it falls marginally below my ass; arguably I'm covered up.

"You okay in there?" I shout as I make my way to the laundry room.

"Stupid...shitty...annoying door. Argh!"

I lean on the doorframe and smile as I watch Ethan pressing every available button while simultaneously yanking on the machine door with no avail. Our clothes are piled at his feet, and I let out a small giggle as he kicks the side of the washer then hops and grabs at his toes. He lets out a string of expletives that run from one to the next in one long cuss.

"Shitfuckerassholepissingcocksuckingdouchenozzle!"

I throw my head back and release a completely undignified snort as he whirls around and narrows his gaze.

"I'm glad my pain amuses you."

I want to try to smooth my features, but holding in my amusement is harder than I thought. I'm straining the muscles in my face with the effort to get my words out without collapsing into hysterics.

"What are you doing?"

"What does it look like I'm doing? Trying to get this damn machine to open so I can wash our stinking wet clothes!"

"Oh." A small giggle escapes me and his gaze narrows further. I scoot past him and press the power switch illuminating all the buttons and then press 'Door'. It pops open, and I turn and smile.

"Always helps if you have the thing turned on first."

"Pfft, whatever. This is a chick's job anyway."

The amusement I was feeling is instantly replaced with a sudden urge to junk-punch him.

"Aw, poor Ethan…in a mood because he couldn't figure out the washer?" I mock in my sweetest baby voice.

I don't get to enjoy the expression he pulls because I'm instantly hit in the face with a pile of dirty socks and boxers.

"Ew…that's gross; you're such a moron! You'd better run."

He laughs until he registers that I'm not joking. His hands fly up to his chest, palms facing up as he takes a step backward.

"It was a joke…Blair, don't you dare!" His voice has lowered to a warning as he watches the box of soap powder I'm poised to throw.

"What was that? Did you just dare me?"

"Okay, okay…I'm sorry, put the box down. I shouldn't have thrown my dirty laundry at you. Tossing a box of suds at me is only gonna…"

I smile triumphantly as he's covered with a heavy dousing of powder before he finishes his sentence. He coughs and shakes his head, causing a flurry of tiny white flakes to tumble from his hair and shoulders like a little snowstorm.

"Mature!" he spits out.

"Hey, you started it, mister."

He rubs his hand over himself, trying to dust down, and I grin.

"Truce?"

"Not even close. I'll get you back, just wait."

I would laugh but his expression is slightly menacing, and now I'm a little worried.

I help him load the washer and we return to fix the mess in the family room. I can feel his eyes burning into the back of me as I'm on all fours, rubbing the coffee stain off the sofa cushion and carpet. It's silent except for the scratching noise the sponge makes against the chocolate-brown fabric. I can feel the atmosphere transforming around me and the room suddenly feels much colder;

there's a sense of an impending confrontation hanging thickly in the air. I give up on the scrubbing and fall to my ass on the carpet, leaning against the sofa as I peel off the rubber gloves I'm wearing. I gather the bottles of stain remover and fabric deodorizer into a neat pile at my side and look up to see him watching me.

"What?" I ask.

"Nothing."

"Liar!"

He smirks and sits down next to me.

"It freaks me out how well you do that."

"Do what?"

"Sense when I'm lying."

"Yeah...you'd think you'd stop doing it, knowing that I can tell a mile off."

He nods his head in contemplation, and his face is somber again.

"I remember."

I look at him blankly, waiting for him to continue.

"Mom, telling me that I'm not hers. I remember it. That's what I was dreaming about before I knocked your drink."

"Oh." I'm not sure what to say to him. I'm relieved as hell that he can recall it, but sad too.

"I told you at the beach?"

"Yeah, you did. We were supposed to be at the movies; you didn't show."

"I called you and you came out, right? Then we drove to the beach, and I told you why I was late."

I nod my head in confirmation and he exhales loudly.

"I know I shouldn't be mad at you but I am. I can't

help it. I don't understand why you would pretend to me like that never happened, even if it was my mom's idea."

I can feel my pulse rise and my palms begin to sweat. I hate how quickly the sadness has crept into his eyes.

"I'm so sorry. I shouldn't have agreed to keep it quiet, but what was I supposed to do? You didn't remember me. You'd just been through the crash; you're dealing with your dad. I couldn't exactly walk into your room and be all, 'Hey I'm Blair, your girlfriend that you don't remember and this over here is your fake mom who's been lying to you for the last eighteen years, just so you know!'"

Her gasp startles Ethan and me as we turn to see Moira standing, case in hand, behind us.

Shit!

Chapter 22

Ethan

"YOU'RE BACK EARLIER than I expected."

"You don't say! I'm going to go put this case away. Why don't you two go and get dressed?" With that Mom turns and exits the room.

"Oh my gosh! I can't believe she just heard all of that, and that she saw me wearing just your t-shirt!" Blair whisper-shouts, her face twisted with embarrassment. "She's going to think we were having sex!"

"Relax, she doesn't care. Come upstairs, I'll grab you some sweats."

I help her up, and she pulls at the hem of the t-shirt, trying to stretch it further down over her legs. The more she pulls at the front, the higher it rides at the back. I let her walk in front of me as we ascend the stairs, purely to enjoy the view as her ass bounces on each step.

She rushes into my room so as not to bump into my mom, and I dig around in my closet until I find a clean pair of sweats for her. She slips them on, and I laugh. She looks like a clown; the material drowns her. She needs to roll the waistband over three times to get them to stay up and it's weirdly sexy. I pull out a dark blue hoody and zip it half way, pushing the sleeves to my elbows, Blair watches me like I'm performing heart surgery or some shit, not getting dressed. I grab her hand and pull her silently back downstairs to go face my mom.

This should be interesting.

Mom returns with a hot drink and sits facing us in the chair opposite the sofa. Blair is fidgeting by my side, wringing her hands together and looking like she would rather be any place than here right now.

"Maybe I should go and let you two talk," Blair announces, and Mom smiles and nods.

"No. I want to hear what the pair of you have to say," I say, before Blair has a chance to get up. Mom's face falls and Blair's pales.

"Go ahead Mom, you flew back to talk, so talk." I sound like a jackass, even to myself, but I've given up caring right now. I sit forward, hands clasped in front of me, my elbows resting on my knees. She looks so tired and sad. I almost feel sorry for her. Only almost.

"Sweetheart, I—"

"Cut the pleasantries, Mom. I remember our conversation. That's not what's even bothering me anymore. Sure, it hurts like a bitch to realize that the person you've been calling Mom your whole life actually isn't your mother at all. But you know what? It's not even having to go through that twice that has me pissed. It's that you tried to hide it, and then had my goddamn girlfriend hide it from me too. Why, Mom? Why?"

She places her drink by her feet and looks pleadingly at me. "I didn't want to stress you out. I thought I was protecting you."

"FROM WHAT?"

"From yourself! Jesus, Ethan, do you think that I haven't noticed what your dad has put you through? Do you think I don't know that you hate me for letting him? I couldn't bear telling you again. We've broken you enough, damn it!" She throws her hands up to her face while sobs wrack her frail body, and all I can do is sit stunned and watch. "I couldn't put that kind of pressure on you two minutes after waking from a coma that left someone dead and your dad paralyzed."

I'm conscious of Blair rubbing my arm and I look down, watching her hand run over my skin before I realize I'm shaking.

"You should have told me."

"I know. But sweetheart, I swear the only reason I didn't was out of love, nothing more. I didn't dare put you through anything else, Ethan—a person can only take so much before they snap. Trust me, I know."

I stand and both sets of eyes follow me as I walk toward the door.

"Don't leave," Blair sighs. It's barely audible but I hear her fine. I have the strangest feeling that I could pick out her voice, even at a whisper, in a stadium full of people shouting.

"I'm just going to get a soda. I'll be right back." With that I leave and go collect a can from the fridge. I'm not in the least bit thirsty, but I didn't want either of them to see me cry. My eyes are stinging as I try hold on to the tears. I don't know what's happening to me. Maybe Mom was right; maybe a person can only take so much. Maybe I've just hit my limit.

ele

It's funny how random things like making a sandwich or hearing a song can trigger memories. I've spent most of the evening listening to Mom defend her actions about lying to me—or as she likes to dress it up, it wasn't lying, it was omitting.

Blair and I came up to my room, and she's been withdrawn and quiet. The atmosphere in here was pretty bleak, so I scrolled through my iPod, hit play and suddenly, BAM! I'm transported in my memory to the reception area of the police department with Blair...

Dad burns holes into my back with his scowl as we finish signing the paperwork. I can't believe he came all this way to bail us out. He's definitely going to make me pay for it the first chance he gets. He looks utterly furious; his arms are crossed over his chest, and his gaze is narrowed. He glances from me to Blair and then back to me again with nothing but disappointment and anger in his eyes. There's no 'hello,' no 'how are you?' No pleasantries at all. He turns and walks out, expecting us to follow silently, and that's exactly what we do.

Blair has my hand in a death grip as we walk towards what I'm assuming is a rental car. Dad opens the back door and stands aside to let us both in. His jaw is working back and forth, and I'm sure that if I were alone right now he wouldn't be so quiet. Blair climbs in, and he closes the door, stopping me from following.

"You've got some explaining to do once your girl-friend's gone," he tells me in an eerily calm voice.

"Yes, sir," I answer and make my way around to the other side of the vehicle and get in. We drive for a little while before Dad finally cracks.

"What the hell happened? I'm dying to know why I had to get on a plane and come bail your sorry ass out of jail. You'd better have a damn good explanation." His voice cuts through the already frigid atmosphere in the car and I see Blair tense from the corner of my eye.

"It was my fault, Mr. Jamison. A guy came onto me at the bar and Ethan was just trying to protect me." My head snaps to Blair's and she's pleading me with her eyes to go along with her story. She's trying to protect me and as much as I love her for doing it, I hate that she feels like she needs to.

"Do I look stupid to you, girl? I was talking to Ethan!" he barks out and Blair flinches back in her seat.

"Don't talk to her like that." I can handle him talking to me like I'm a piece of shit but not her. Never her.

"Who the hell do you think you're talking to? I've just come to bail you and your little whore out, and this is how you talk to me?"

I see red and ball my fists at my side. "If you ever call her a whore again I swear to god I'll make you regret it." My words filter into the calm and quiet of the car, but they hit their mark as intended. The road we're on is empty, so he pulls to a stop and turns in his seat with eyes blazing like fire. I know what's coming next; at least I would if we weren't all strapped into a car. This would be the point where he loses his shit and beats the crap out of me until he feels better. Thing is, he can't do that from where he's sitting, and he's not the kind of guy that likes an audience. Blair's eyes are wide as she takes in the stalemate that we've come to.

"What the hell did you just say to me?"

"You fucking heard me! Don't disrespect her and talk down to her. Your problem is with me, no one else. And you know what? My whole life I've wondered why you seem to hate me so much, put me down, make me feel worthless. Well, now I know. Mom told me about my real mom. What kind of a man does that make you, huh? I'm the only thing you've got left of a woman you supposedly loved, and what do you do? You beat me. Your own flesh and blood; part of you and her. Most people would cherish the only reminder of a person they once loved, but oh no, not you, Dad. No, you preferred to kick and punch and beat the hell out of me for reminding you of her. I can't help how I look, or mannerisms that I may share with her. I've never intentionally tried to bait you or upset you. I've spent my whole fucking life trying to live up to what you expected, and it was never going to be good enough, was it? Because what it all boils down to is that you hate me. You hate me for living and reminding you of what you've lost. I'm never going to be able to change that, am I?"

"Get out of the car, now!"

I look to Blair who's shaking her head.

"Guys, you need to calm down," she pleads as we both unbuckle and make a move to exit the car. That's

when I see the look of pure horror flash across her face. I hear her scream just as I turn to see the truck heading straight for us and showing no sign of stopping. I throw myself across her to unbuckle her belt, and then darkness.

It's as much as I recall before waking up in the hospital. The realization hits that it's my fault that we stopped in the middle of the road arguing, and I lunge off the bed and into my bathroom. I barely make it to the toilet before my stomach empties and the guilt creeps in, consuming my whole body and pushing out everything else.

"Ethan, what's wrong? Baby, are you okay?"

Blair looks as panicked as I feel. She rushes to the sink and dampens a washcloth, placing it on the back of my neck.

"You completely zoned out on me and then started shaking. I thought you were having some sort of seizure."

I want to answer her, but I don't trust my voice not to break. I let go of my grip on the toilet and raise a hand, trying to indicate that I need a second.

The cold cloth she has pressed on me is dripping beads of icy water down my back and making me shiver. I pull it from her grasp without saying a word and reposition it on my forehead as I twist around and lean my back against the wall. She's knelt in front of me now, and the worry in her eyes does nothing but add to the mountain of blame I feel take up residence on my shoulders.

"You want me to get you some water?"

What I want is for this nightmare to end, but I can't exactly ask for that.

"I'm not thirsty," I clip, and I'm pretty sure I couldn't

keep anything down at the moment anyway. My stomach is still in knots.

"You wanna tell me what this is all about? 'Cause I'm going to be honest with you here, Ethan, you're starting to freak me out. Should I go get your mom?"

"No!" I blurt out. "I'll be okay in a minute. I didn't mean to worry you. I'm fine."

"'I'm fine' is the universal code for anything but fine. I'm a girl, I should know. Please…just talk to me."

I can't look her in the eye. My dad…the trucker…her operation…it's all my fault.

"I remembered the crash," I mumble, focusing my attention on the tiny cracks in the glaze of the ceramic tiles on the bathroom floor. There are millions of seemingly insignificant hairline fractures, barely visible until you look hard enough. The tiles themselves look almost flawless from a distance, but if you tried to remove one, it would crumble. Those fractures have all played a part in weakening the hard exterior. One firm knock and it would be irreparable, leaving the person who delivered the blow stunned wondering how one seamlessly uneventful knock could destroy the whole thing. I feel like that tile.

"What exactly did you remember?" she asks, but the sound of her voice tells me that she already knows.

I take a deep breath and then tell her what I remembered from the police station leading up to arguing with my dad. "I should have stayed quiet until we got back home. Why did I choose that moment to finally say something? It's because of me that we stopped the car; it's all because of me."

Her arms fold around me, and she holds me like she

knows I'm about to disintegrate.

"It's not your fault; none of this is your fault. Your dad, Ethan, he's the one that treated you bad, he's the one that started the argument that day, and ultimately, he's the one that stopped the car—not you. You can't blame yourself for this, for any of it."

I want so badly to believe her, to kiss her and look into those beautiful dark emerald eyes, and tell her that I know she's speaking the truth. But I can't, because it isn't. I'm as much to blame for that accident as he is. He may have stopped the car, but it was me that drove him to do it.

"Baby?"

I can hear her heart beating through the cotton of my t-shirt. My head's pushed tightly against her chest as her hands draw small lazy circles across my shoulders and back. I don't want to move. I don't want to deal. I just want to stay here and let myself forget that my life isn't a bowl full of cherries.

"Yeah?"

"You're still shivering. Come get into bed."

Her arms fall as I push up and take her hands to help her stand. She walks backward, never letting her focus drop from me as she pulls me over to my bed, throws the comforter back and climbs in. I slip in beside her, tuck my face into her neck and shoulder, and then breathe her in. Neither one of us sleeps; instead, we hold on to each other in silence. Blair is facing away from the door, and at one point I notice it crack and my mom peer in. I instantly close my eyes in fake slumber. I'm not ready to face anything else today. I wait until finally I hear footsteps on the stairs before I press myself deeper against Blair and try to make sense of this mess.

Chapter 23

Blair

MONDAY ROLLS AROUND entirely too quickly. The morning sun is warming my face through the cracks in my curtains, and when I turn to shield my eyes I notice that my cell is already lit up with a message from Ethan, I left his house late Saturday night and spent all day Sunday with my mom at home. It was good to have a day where I could just process my thoughts and not have to deal with anything else, as selfish as it sounds. I needed that time. I think Ethan and Moira needed some time too. My mom was amazing but then, she's always amazing. I had a complete meltdown at one point, and she listened to me vent without judgment. I'm not your typical talker; I like time to prepare my thoughts and ideas on the situation at hand, and attempt to have it clear in my mind before voicing anything about it. But I can always count on her to be right there when I do decide I want to confide in someone.

I wish Ethan had that.

I'm desperate to convince him that seeing a therapist would be a good thing. My mom agrees, but it has to be his decision. Ultimately, he needs to be the one to decide that talking to somebody is the right thing for him to do. I don't want to push him; if I'm honest, I don't dare. I think if he had a chance to sit down and talk with his Dad that might help too. Their relationship is so screwed up, I think gaining some closure would benefit him, but I don't see that in their future anytime soon and it scares me. If Frank doesn't make it through his surgery and the two of them don't talk, it will always be an unresolved issue, an open wound that won't heal.

I reach out and snatch the phone from my nightstand.

From: Ethan
Pick you up for school? X

I'm about to text back 'yes' until I notice the time and realize I'm going to be late if I don't get my ass into gear. I reply that I'll meet him there and then take the quickest shower of my life. I throw my green *Obey gravity it's the law* tank on with my skinnies and chucks, leaving my hair down to air dry and skipping breakfast to make it to school before the first bell.

It's times like this when I miss being invisible. I used to be able to walk these halls and not a single person other than Em would register my presence. Now, not so much. Everyone in this school is aware of Ethan Jamison, and by default, Ethan Jamison's girlfriend—although I don't think any of them could actually tell you my name. That's what happens with couples: the less popular of the two loses what identity they had, no matter how obscure. I'm no longer Blair to these students; I'm Ethan's girl. There are exceptions, though; some of them have bothered to find out who I am, no doubt in an attempt to make false allegiances with him and his friends. Everyone wants to be friends with the popular kids and I must look like an easy 'in' to them.

I weave my way in and out of the crowded hallway while replying to a bunch of *hello's* and *how are you's* from people I've never spoken to before. It's awkward when strangers make conversation with you or use your name, and you have no clue of theirs. Emily would have loved watching me panic. I've always had the socially inept 'please don't approach me' vibe down pat. I perfected it after *Billygate*, as Em used to so affectionately refer to it. I smile at the memory.

We were at lunch one day in middle school. I'd never really had a crush on anyone before, but I'd stupidly confided in my so-called best friend that I thought Corry Spencer and Billy Greenwood were cute. Em in her infinite wisdom had told Billy that I liked him, and what happened next defined what has until recently become my high school career when it comes to interacting with others.

Em noticed Billy making his way over to our lunch table first and kicked my leg, nodding in his direction. I looked up, and his eyes were zeroed in on me. He waved and I looked around, certain he was making his way over to someone else, but no, the salutation was for me. Before I could stop myself I gave one of those awkward finger wiggle waves that you see all the airheads do in movies.

He straddled the bench right next to me, never shifting his gaze, and I could feel myself turning beet red. Em jabbed me in the back, prompting me to say hello, and I was greeted by a huge toothy sparkling white grin. Seriously, this kid could have done toothpaste commercials. I almost expected a little light to flash in his teeth and make a ping sound.

He didn't say anything right away, and it threw me. I picked up my Coke to busy myself, to avoid sitting and staring at him like a moron. He leaned in close, too close as it turned out, and asked if I wanted to go to the movies with him. His timing sucked, or maybe it was mine, because I'd just taken a huge gulp of soda. He took me by complete surprise, and I think I gasped but that's a lot harder than it sounds with your mouth full. The drink hit the back of my throat and I immediately choked. I threw my hand over my mouth to do damage control, but the soda needed out. It sprayed through my nose and the fizzy burn it caused made me open my mouth, which my fingers did a poor job of guarding. Coke spilled out all over me. If anyone around us thought he looked horrified at it, they hadn't seen anything yet. I coughed and spluttered, gasping for air while trying to say sorry. I remember thinking 'thank god it didn't spray him'.

Em began slapping my back to try and help me—at least that's what she told me later—and it thrust me forward abruptly. That's when it happened. It was like time slowed down, and everyone turned to see what the commotion was right as my retainer propelled from my mouth in a trajectory set for Billy Greenwood's lap. I watched in utter disbelief as it landed in his crotch, covered in my sa-

*liva and Coke. He fished it up on instinct, then his face
pinched and contorted as he realized what he was holding.
The whole table began laughing as he dropped it like it
was infected with Anthrax, and it landed in someone's Ce-
sar salad. He stood up and told me that he'd just remembered he couldn't take me to the movies because he forgot
about an assignment that he had to hand in and then bolt-
ed from the cafeteria. Em was trying to console me while
also trying to calm her own hysterics. The whole incident
pretty much put me off talking to anyone at school for
months. After that I did my best to blend into the background.*

I can still see her in my mind's eye, trying not to
laugh, and it warms my heart and then breaks it a little.

I miss her.

I round the corner to see a semicircle of girls gathered
around where Ethan's waiting at my locker. Casey and
Brie stand on either side of him, like super tiny pissed off
bodyguards; the girls are all clamoring for his attention
and offering up condolences about his dad. They're not
doing anything wrong but Brie looks like she's about to
cut someone when a girl with long red hair leans in and
whispers something into Ethan's ear. His face pales and
then he notices me, noticing him. His expression flashes
from relief to alarm at seeing me in less than a second. My
step falters and then the redhead turns and my stomach
flips. I paste on a fake ass grin and carry on with my approach. Della looks like a cat with the cream as she watches me approach. She flips her hair and turns to say something to the girl beside her before they both look over at

ELLE BROOKS

me and then let out a laugh. Ethan pushes past her and she teeters on her high heels and stumbles against her friend as he moves her out of his path. He emerges through the small crowd and picks me up mid-stride, twirling me around before placing a kiss on my nose and popping me back on the ground. I'm in no doubt that this is his attempt at quashing the rumors Della has been working hard to circulate in our absence. But I love him for it.

"Morning, Princess. You're a sight for sore eyes."

"More like a sight to make your eyes sore," Della says behind her hand, loud enough for the whole crowd to hear. There are a few sniggers and then a hush. I look over to see Casey holding Brie back. Their eyes meet mine and I know instantly they are waiting for me to respond, as are the rest of them.

I don't want to rise to the bait, so instead I ignore them and Ethan squeezes my hand and smiles. I open my locker as Della sashays around the students loitering in the hall and advances in our direction with half of the group hot on her heels. She passes by and flashes me a huge smug smile.

"See you around, superstar," she drawls to Ethan before dropping her voice to a whisper.

"Later loser," she chortles and I have to suppress my inner twelve-year-old to not stick my foot out and send the bitch tumbling on her ass.

"Oh, by the way Ethan, I think I have a pair of your shades. You left them in my bedroom the last time you were there," she calls over her shoulder and I can feel the red mist descend over me.

"Congratulations, Della! You're officially a bigger attention-seeking whore in person than you are on Facebook. That's some achievement! Your folks must be real proud," I call. It's catty and immature, but it feels so good to watch her face lose the smug expression she's always wearing. Her scowl is instant.

"Whatever, geek! If you weren't such a nerd, maybe you'd have a chance at keeping your boyfriend."

Ethan's head whips around and he's about to respond but I get there first.

"I'm sorry, but I find it hard to take someone seriously when their favorite shade of lip gloss is dick. Spread all the rumors you want, Della, if it makes you feel better. I trust my boyfriend, and nothing you can dream up in that empty head of yours will make me doubt that."

People are hollering and some idiot jock is chanting 'catfight' somewhere in the background. Della looks furious and stutters trying to form a comeback. I ignore her and throw my bag into my locker as Ethan leans down close.

"This may not be the right time...but that was hot! I like you feisty." He laughs and takes my hand as Brie and Casey stand open-mouthed looking at me.

"What?" I glare at them and ask.

"Nothing," Brie, answers wide-eyed.

"Damn, I hope someone caught that on camera," Casey says with a huge grin. "Favorite shade of lip gloss is dick! Oh my god, her face was so mad!"

"I'm not exactly proud of stooping to her level, but I'm sick of her being mean to me for no reason."

Ethan stays quiet, but his fingers slip through mine as he stands by my side, tucking me under his arm.

"Well, she needed bringing down a peg or two. I'm glad you did it," Brie tells me before she excitedly—and by excited I mean bouncing on her toes and clapping—announces that her parents have agreed to buy her a new car. It's apparently a graduation present/going away to college present.

"You already have a car?" Casey says, confused, and Brie stops dead.

"Please...it's almost as old as I am; they wouldn't buy me a brand new one until I could prove that I can drive it without incident."

"Um, yeah...but you've bumped it parking at least twice a week since you got your license."

"Hello...that was parking it, not *driving* it. Plus, Daddy doesn't need to know that."

Ethan shakes his head; I'm not sure if its' in amusement or alarm, while Casey and I look at one and other and burst out laughing. The bell sounds just as Brie spots Jackson, and we each make our way to class.

ele

The rest of the day runs smoothly: there's no drama with Della, Dannii doesn't acknowledge me and Ethan acts like nothing has happened, and it freaks me out. Monday night he has a hospital appointment which he brushes off with, 'It went fine' when he picks me up for school Tuesday morning. *I hate the word fine!* The day pans out much the same as the one before, and Ethan has music practice after school for the rest of the week to catch up on missed time. Wednesday follows suit with the fake *everything is rosy* routine, and I finally can't take any more by Thursday at lunch time.

"Don't lie to me—everything is not fine. Please stop saying fine! Ugh."

"What do you want me to say, Princess? I don't get it …I don't know what you're expecting. If you thought I'd come back to school and be crying in the halls because of my broken home and fucked up life, you're wrong. It's never gonna happen. I'm okay!"

I want to scream at how infuriating he's being. We are in the library, our textbooks open, going over math, and he hasn't heard a single word I've spoken to him in the last half hour. I'm not sure he's heard a single word I've spoken to him this past week. He's slipped into a robotic, anesthetized version of himself. Yeah, sure, he's doing an excellent job of being the Mr. Charming everyone expects, but I can see it's an act.

"I don't expect anything, it just seems like you're putting on this phony persona with everyone, including me, and I don't like it."

"Baby, I might give the rest of this town what they expect to see, but not you. You're the only person who gets the real me," he says with a wink. "So stop worrying your cute little butt about it."

He drags my chair closer and the noise ricochets around the room like a bomb has just been detonated. He winces and smiles at me as Mrs. Phelps, the librarian, attempts to terrify us with her evil glare, and it works. Ethan squeezes my thighs and leans over to whisper in my ear. "She won't be able to hear us if you want to take a quick trip behind the stalls in the ancient philosophy section?"

He sits back, wearing a huge grin, and it actually looks real and not the artificial ones he's been shooting people last week.

"Okay," I utter behind my hand, trying to disguise what I'm saying. It's not like Mrs. Phelps would be able to lip read from so far away, the woman wears glasses with three-inch thick lenses and still squints when she's talking to you.

"What? Seriously?" he asks in astonishment. There's a little hope laced into his voice, and he's looking at me like he's waiting for me to shout 'joke!'

"Seriously, you have no idea how many fantasies I've had about fooling around in the library."

His eyes narrow and he's studying my face. "You've had fantasies about me in the library."

"No, I said I'd fantasized about fooling around in the library, but I didn't mention you."

"Wounded." He clutches his chest in mock heart-break. "You're gonna have to be punished for that." He shoots me a lopsided grin, and his dimples appear as he grabs my hand and we navigate our way to the back of the library.

"I'm surprised you even know where the ancient phi-losophy section is," I mock as we walk down row after row of dusty old bookshelves.

"It's in the makeout section; of course, I know where it is," he throws back casually and my feet immediately come to a halt.

"You're leading me back here to where you've taken someone else?" I almost shout, and he laughs at my scowl.

"Shush, you don't want Phelpzilla to come find us.

No Blair, you're the first person I'm leading back here."
He raises his hand. "Scout's honor."

"If you expect me to believe you were a scout, you're delusional."

"You're right; I wasn't a scout, but I promise you're the only girl I've brought here. I don't think I've ever been in this library before I met you."

I let out a little huff but secretly I'm relieved. The thought of Ethan with other girls is one I try to keep firmly out of mind. I like the fact that he's bringing me here, and it's a first. I follow him until we're huddled into a quiet, dark corner. He spins me around and his lips land against mine before I know what's hit me. His muscular frame is pushed up against me, pinning my back against the bookshelf, his arms caging me in. I moan into his mouth as his tongue lightly traces the seam of my lips before delving in and tasting me. My adrenaline spikes and the prospect of someone catching us excites me more than I thought possible. Just knowing there are people going about their day only feet away has me rubbing my legs together, trying to quell the hunger Ethan is eliciting. I can feel the delicious stirs resonating within the depths of my stomach and it's all I can do to quiet the embarrassingly loud groans fighting to get out of my chest. His hands cup my face gently before beginning a slow and meticulous descent towards my chest, palming my breasts and driving me insane. He knows what he's doing; he has a wicked gleam in his eyes as he moves his lips from my mouth to the spot under my jaw. I'm confident I sigh as he trails hot wet kisses down my neck and bites gently at my shoulder. I'm so consumed with the feel of him against me that I fling my arms back and send books crashing to the floor.

Ethan's head snaps back up.

"Are you trying to get us caught, Ms. Thomas?"

The way my name rolls of his tongue is so low and gravelly, I think he could probably get me off just talking to me.

"Sorry, you're kind of making me lose my mind."

Anyone would think he'd just won the lotto; the smile that overtakes him is smoldering, and he looks pretty smug with himself.

"Princess, I need you so badly right now."

"Yeah...I think that we need to get the hell out of here and finish this."

"We're not going anywhere yet," he says pushing his hand under my shirt and tracing along the cup of my bra before he tugs it down slightly and pinches my nipple. The shock sends a wave of heat straight to my core, and I have to focus on staying upright. I move my hand and run it over the front of his jeans; he's straining against the fabric, and it makes me smile to know that I'm affecting him just as much as he is me. His hands run down my body and snake around my back, pulling me tight to his chest while he squeezes and kneads my ass. I revel in the feel of his fingers pushing into my skin. It's at the point of painful pleasure, and I think I'll die if he doesn't help me release some of this pent-up sexual frustration. Apparently I've turned into a brazen harlot. Sex at school is something I would never have dreamed of in a thousand years. However, I'm pretty sure Ethan could talk me into it with very little effort right now. *God, who am I, and what happened to the quiet nerd?*

"Blair?" his voice is strangled as I realize I've inadvertently moved his hand to the apex of my thighs.

I want to respond, but the only thing I can manage to do right now is pant into his mouth as his kisses rain down on me.

His hand moves higher, and I'm momentarily embarrassed that he's pulling away until I feel the skin-on-skin contact of his fingers slipping underneath the waistband of my jeans and panties. He leans back to look at me, his eyes are seeking permission and there's no way I'm not granting it. I watch in delight as his mouth quirks at the side, and he lets go of my ass with his other hand to put his finger up to his mouth and shush me. *I'm done for.*

His fingers slide inside of me so slowly that I have to squeeze my whole body in an attempt to not cry out in ecstasy. He begins moving them unhurriedly, letting my excitement build, and then my eyes snap open as I hear voices approach. I look up at Ethan, panicked, and attempt to move, but he has the most wicked gleam in his eyes as he holds me in place and ups his tempo.

"Nice and quiet baby," he commands, and I feel myself growing closer to the edge. I'm rattled and turned on as hell. My body begins to tense at my impending orgasm, and he muffles my moans with his mouth, swallowing my cries and heightening the hedonistic wave that consumes me.

I'm pinned to the bookcase, and if Ethan moves, I'll collapse like the spent mass of limbs and boneless flesh that he's reduced me to. My eyes flutter before his beautiful face comes back into focus, just in time for me to witness him pull his hand slowly out of my pants and taste his fingers.

Holy shit!

I feel my jaw fall slacken as he steps back and winks at me leaning here, dazed, confused, and completely sated.

"It's just above your head, Blair," he says as he reaches for Plato's *The Last Days of Socrates.*

I'm about to ask what he's been smoking, just as Mrs. Phelps rounds the corner with a student and stops short in front of us.

Oh.

My.

Gosh!

I instantly feel my cheeks ignite, and I mumble my thanks to Ethan, grabbing the book and bolting. He catches up, sniggering at my complete mortification and I elbow him in the side.

"Ouch, just recovering from a car accident…remember," he breathes in a strained voice, before he laughs as I quicken my pace. "Blair." He reaches out and grabs the hem of my t-shirt, pulling me back until I bump into him.

"Relax, no one heard or saw anything except me."

I feel my shoulders drop slightly, and I blow out a long breath. He kisses my temple and laces our fingers together as we walk back to the desks to collect our things. Him with a confident, cocky spring to his step, and me on shaky newborn foal legs.

Chapter 24

Ethan

I'M SURE IT isn't normal for a hard on to be this painful. Seriously, the look on Blair's face while I made her come in the library is seared into my brain; I can't stop picturing her face and the way she clung to me. I've been hard for the last twenty minutes solid, which wouldn't be a problem if we weren't in the middle of a math class. We were assigned seating at the beginning of the year and I'm between two football players, so sitting here with a tent in my pants is less than ideal. Just knowing she's somewhere at the back of the room is driving me insane. I've regressed to a horny pre-teen, and when I look down to my notes, I notice that I've inadvertently drawn a pair of tits in the bottom left hand corner of the page. I need to get a grip, or get laid. Preferably the second. I'm mid-fantasy when my cell starts to ring. I typically don't have it on silent; Professor Hillman looks like he wants to throw daggers at me as my ringtone blasts out through the otherwise quiet room.

"Mr. Jamison, need I remind you that this is a class-room? You should be well aware of the rules concerning cell phones by now. Turn it off. Immediately."

The class fills with sniggering and people take the opportunity to talk to their friends at the disruption. Hillman's pissed as he threatens detention to anyone else that makes a noise.

Great.

His eyes are still set on me, so I nod and switch my phone off completely; the last thing I need is for it to go off again and land my ass in any more trouble.

The hour seems to run so slowly it's borderline torturous. I have no interest in what's being taught. All I can concentrate on is getting the hell out of here and dragging Blair home with me to finish what we started in the library. The bell sounds and I pack up my books, take out my cell and all but run out of the classroom into the hall where she's waiting.

"Who was calling in the middle of class?" she asks.

"I didn't see; I turned it off without looking," I say, turning my cell on and waiting for it to power up.

"I'm surprised that he went so easy on you; I've seen him freak at people for far less than having their cells on."

"Hmm, what?" I look up, and she's studying the phone with a curious expression.

"What's wrong?"

"Not sure. My mom's called me like six times, and texted, telling me to call her ASAP."

I watch as her face drops, and I know she's thinking the same thing I am; that something has happened with my dad. *I should only be so lucky*. I hit call and mom answers on the second ring.

"Hey, you've been calling—what's up?"

"Hi, sweetheart. The hospital has been on the phone; your dad has contracted pneumonia, and they want me to head back. It's…well, oh, Ethan, it's not looking good. I need to catch a flight tonight. Can you come home? I…I have some things I want to talk through with you, and I don't want to do it over the phone."

Fantastic; no doubt there'll be more revelations to add to the clusterfuck that is our life. I don't want to upset her more than she already sounds. The last thing I want to do is get into an argument with her over the phone in the middle of the school.

"Sure, I'll be home soon."

I disconnect the call, and Blair is already leading me out towards the parking lot.

"Did you hear that?" I ask as we step out into the warm breeze. I squint trying to get my eyes to adjust to the light.

"Yeah, come on, I'm coming with you. We need to get out of here quickly before any of my teachers see me ditch."

"You don't have to co—"

"Don't you dare tell me not to come. I'm not arguing about this; I'm in this with you. Now, do you want me to drive?"

"Hell no, Princess. No disrespect, but your driving is scarier than the prospect of what awaits me at home," I say in a joking tone, and she flips me off.

"Such a lady, Ms. Thomas."

"Bite me, Mr. Jamison."

"Is that an invitation?" There's genuine hope in my voice, and she shakes her head in disgust.

"There's something wrong with you!"

"Yeah, you're only figuring this now. Ain't you supposed to be smart?" I say as I tap her ass and she almost jumps out of her skin.

"Maybe I'm a glutton for punishment," she sing-songs and attempts to wink. It's equal parts funny and cute; she looks like she has something in her eye and is pulling a face that's a lot less than attractive. I think I've just discovered the one thing she doesn't seem to be any good at, and it makes me love her even more.

elle

I'm stunned. I have no idea on what planet she could think that this is a good idea. It's the last thing I want to do, and Blair agreeing with her has me thrown entirely.

"Ethan, please. Honey this may be your last chance. He requested that I ask you."

"There's no way I'm going to see him, Mom. Jesus, have you forgotten the reception I got the last time I tried to see him in the hospital? He freaked. I can't believe you're even asking this of me."

"Baby," Blair interrupts and fixes me with a steady gaze. "I really think that you should consider it. It might give you closure. If not, at least you won't go through life regretting not saying what you wanted to him, or asking him the questions burning at the back of your mind. I know it's a totally different scenario, but I never got the chance to say goodbye to my father, and I wish every day that I had. Because the last words I ever spoke to him were a complaint that he'd woken me up too early. If I'd had any idea that he was going to suffer a massive heart attack that morning, there are so many things I would have told him. Whether the things you want to say to your dad are good or bad, make sure that you can live with the decision never to speak them."

I rest my head in my hands and curse the fact that I know she's right. I don't want to see him, at all. But that's only how I feel at this point in time. Who knows how I'd feel later on?

"Okay."

"Okay, what?" Mom and Blair both say in unison.

"I'll come with you," I say to Mom and her eyes instantly well. Blair looks over and mouths I love you. It doesn't make the feeling of nausea at talking to the asshole go away, but it does give me a strange sense of peace every time she speaks those words to me.

"I'll book us on the six-thirty flight. I'm not sure how long we'll be staying, so pack for a few days, okay?"

A few days—shit. I thought I'd get there, talk to him and fly back the same night.

"Come on, Princess, you can help me pack."

We get to my room and Blair closes the door before pushing me down onto my bed and straddling my lap. I'd be way more excited about our position if she weren't looking at me like she felt sorry for me.

"I'm proud of you for doing this; I just wanted you to know that," she says as she pushes me backward and rests her head over my heart.

"You know, I could always come with you if you wanted me to."

"I love that you offered, but I think I'd rather do this by myself."

She lets out a long soft sigh and asks if I'm sure. I plaster a fake smile on and tell her absolutely; only it's a huge fucking lie, because I've never been more unsure about anything in my whole goddamn life.

Mom shouts up that the flights are booked and that we need to leave within the next two hours. I figure that gives me ten minutes to pack, and the rest of the time to spend fooling around with the sexy little nerd currently lying on top of me.

"You need to call the guys and tell them the score. You should be at practice in an hour," Blair announces, and it's good she did, because it had slipped my mind. Jackson will be pissed; he's keen as hell to get as many hours banked as possible. I think he's still secretly hoping we're going to get signed. Our manager, Sam, seems to think it's a real possibility, and Jackson has pinned all his hopes on me changing my mind about going to Eastman if we do land a contract. I've told him before that college is my priority, and it still is. In fact, the thought is more appealing now than ever before. It will be great to finally leave this place behind.

"I'll call them in a minute; I have something important to do first."

She lifts her head from my chest.

"Like what?"

I flip her and pin her underneath me in one quick movement. She looks completely disorientated, and I take the opportunity to carefully remove her glasses, leaning over and placing them on my cabinet beside me. I push my fingers through her long dark messy hair and lower my mouth to hers. Kissing her is like a drug; the more I do it, the more I need to do it. It's an addiction and I have no intention of kicking the habit. I gently draw her bottom lip into my mouth and suck on it; she has the most amazing lips. They're tantalizingly soft and full and I love that they always have a hint of her cherry lip balm flavor.

I have to force myself to cut the kissing short; it's awakened all my senses, and if I carry on, I'm not going to be able to stop. Which is kind of a problem, seen as how my mom's in the other room. She wriggles underneath me, and I'm instantly hard. Her eyes widen when she realizes this and I groan at the prospect of having to get up, pack and leave her here. I place one last quick kiss on her nose then jump up and head into my bathroom. I need to throw some cold water on myself and get myself sorted. I peer out of the door and can see that Blair's still rested on my bed with her hair draped across my pillows. Yeah, going to need lots and lots of cold water.

Chapter 25

Blair

I'M SITTING IN my car outside Emily's house. I've only been here once since she died, and it felt so wrong to be surrounded by all of her things, and not have her there. I've made excuses to avoid visiting with Pam and Bill, but I know it's not fair of me. I promised Em that I would still come and see her parents, especially her mom. The conversation we had about it is one I'll never forget.

"So I need to ask you a favor. I'm really hoping that you will agree to this because it's probably one of the most important things I'll ever ask you to do," Em tells me as she sets her pumpkin-flavored coffee on the dark wood table of the café and leans back into the huge tan leather sofa we're both lounged on.

"Okay, sounds ominous," I say taking a sip of my hot chocolate and hugging it tight to my chest. "Shoot."

She looked so frail at that point; her cheeks were

sunken, and she'd lost all the plumpness to her skin. The cancer had made her look older, somehow. It couldn't, however, detract from how pretty she was. It was only a couple of months before she died, and her chemo had been stopped. Her hair had begun growing back since her last cycle had finished, and was now a pretty choppy pixie length. It looked good. I'm sure to any passerby she looked like any other teenage girl. Just a painfully thin one.

"I've been worrying about my parents, and my mom in particular. My dad, he's strong. I know that when I go, he'll be the rock that pulls my mom through. It's her that I worry the most about. I hate the thought that she's not going to be a mom anymore an—"

I raised my hand signaling for her to halt, and she rolled her eyes dramatically.

"You'll always be her daughter, even when you're not here. Gosh, Em, she will always be your mother. That doesn't change when someone dies."

I'm not sure what it was that had me so worked up, but hearing her speak those words, they squeezed painfully at my heart so tightly that I wanted to scream.

"Blair, I know that, but my mom lives for me; you know how she is. I'm her whole life, and that scares me more than dying. When the time comes…what will she do? Who will she live for? She gave up work to care for me so it's not like she can immerse herself in that to keep her busy. She's not really in contact with any of her old friends, and all her new ones are cancer moms. I'm pretty confident that she won't be able to keep going into the hospital to meet with them when I die, because it will be too raw for her. That's the last place I'd want to be if it

were me, don't you think?"

I nodded my head but stayed quiet. I knew that if I tried to respond, my voice would crack and I'd be a blubbering mess in the middle of Starbucks.

"I want you to go visit with her sometimes. She's so used to you being at our house; you're a part of our family and I know without a doubt she'd hate it if you stopped seeing her. She thinks of you as a daughter, she always has. You're in all of our family photo albums."

"Of course, I'll visit your parents. You should know that I wouldn't just stop. They're like my second mom and dad. I love them."

"Oh, Blair...thank you."

She ambushed me with a tight hug, and we sat for a long time in that embrace, both trying to hold back our tears.

I feel instantly guilty that I've not come back sooner. The memory of my best friend is the kick I needed, and I unbuckle my belt and jump out of the car before I can give myself time to change my mind.

"Blair, sweetheart!"

Pam's voice booms as she flings the front door open and rushes down the path to intercept me with a squeeze. Her blonde hair is billowing in the breeze and she looks so much like Em that it hurts to see her.

"Hi Pam! How are you?"

"I'm fine, but never mind about me—how are you? Goodness baby girl, when your mom called and told Bill that you'd been involved in that crash...it was awful. We were both so worried about you. I've called Susan every day for an update on you."

"I'm okay; I escaped pretty lightly," I tell her as she steers me into the house that is the setting of so many of my childhood memories. There are pictures on every wall of Em, and I'm in a lot of them too. It feels nice and familiar to see them again. I spend a good two hours talking with Pam about what I've been doing since Em passed. I tell her about Ethan and me. I was a little worried at first; Pam knew all about Em's crush. She seems genuinely happy that we are together, though. It's a weight off my mind that I didn't even realize I was carrying. She tells me all about the volunteer work she's begun at the hospital and the support group that she and another of the moms that has gone through the same thing have set up. I'm so proud of her and I know Emily would be, too. She's doing amazingly well. We both have a moment where we allow our tears to fall as we retell silly stories, and it feels so good to let it out. I'm about to leave when Pam announces that she's started to pack Emily's bedroom up. The thought upsets me. I realize that it needs to be done, and I'm sure it's a lot harder for Pam and Bill to do than it is for me to hear about. It still aches so bad to know I'll never see her again and that this isn't some holiday that she's on. She won't be home soon; it's forever, and it's horrible.

"There are a few things in her room—pictures, journals, etcetera. I can't keep them, but I don't want to just throw them away. Would you want to take a look? Maybe you'd like to have some of them?"

"Yes!" I blurt out. The thought of her things being tossed out doesn't sit well with me at all.

"Okay, sweetheart, why don't you go and have a look

around her bedroom. I'll be in the kitchen when you've finished."

I nod and make my way through the back of the house to her room. I open the door, and I'm hit with the smell of her. It hasn't gone; it lingers as if she were in here only yesterday and it knocks me back. I wasn't expecting it. I sit on her desk chair and stare at her huge lilac room; it looks so bare without her in it. I'm not sure how long I spend looking at her things and reminiscing about every piece I come across, but it feels like a long time. I use one of the storage boxes leaning against the wall and fill it with a pile of old journals. Em was religious about keeping a diary. I tried once; I wrote in it for maybe a week and then lost interest. I'm a reader, not a writer.

I place two pictures of us in the box along with Collin, a threadbare ratty old stuffed dog that she used to cart everywhere when we were in kindergarten. Her dad had to pay her to stop taking it to school. She took it everywhere, and Pam used to have to steal it from her bed at night to wash it. I'm suddenly sad that it wasn't buried with her. I decide that Collin can come live with me. I know Ethan will tease me about it, but I don't care. I check my cell quickly at the thought of him. He'd texted me last night to let me know he'd gotten to Arizona and was planning on visiting with his father today. My tummy twists at how anxious he must be. I know he doesn't want to do it. He told me he would call once he'd spoken with him. I'm still waiting, and the more time that passes the queasier I feel. I really hope that everything went okay.

I say my goodbyes to Pam and promise to check in again when Bill is home. She laughs when she sees Collin peeping out from the box I'm holding. She tells me not to be a stranger as she walks me out to my car and I mentally kick myself for staying away this long. I miss her, and I miss my best friend.

Chapter 26

Ethan

THIS ISN'T WHAT I was expecting; not that I had any pre-conceived notion of what would happen but I'm just thrown, I guess. We arrived after visiting hours last night, so we stayed at the hotel and got some sleep. Well, no, that's a lie; tossed and turned all night wondering what to say to my dad is more accurate. Is it wrong to unleash eighteen years' worth of hurt to someone that might be dying? I spent a long time wondering if I should try being civil, pleasant, and that way if he did die, maybe he would go in peace. The trouble with that scenario is that he'd get to leave thinking that everything is okay, and it's not.

"Mrs. Jamison, and…"

The consultant pauses, giving me time to fill in the blanks.

"Ethan. I'm his son."

"And Ethan, right, of course. I'm not sure what you've been told about Frank's condition, so I'll explain a little of what's happening. Individuals such as your husband and father with a spinal cord injury are at increased risk for developing respiratory complications. Any loss of respiratory muscle control weakens the pulmonary system, no matter what the level of injury is. However, the risk for complications is greater for persons with a complete injury, as is Frank's case. He lacks the ability to breathe without assistance. His lungs have collapsed from the lack of air being drawn into them.

"Now, we have made adjustments and we're able to counter this with his ventilator. However, Frank is now suffering from pneumonia. In cases such as this one, it is the leading cause of death. We have him stable at the moment; he's falling in and out of consciousness and is suffering from delirium. At present, Frank is not what we would consider to be strong enough to withstand the surgery that is needed to re-attach his skull to his spinal column. We have postponed the procedure, but I would urge you to make arrangements in case the worst happens.

"I realize that this is an upsetting time. I'm going to leave you to digest what I've just said. Please feel free to go in and visit with Frank. From what the nurses tell me, he has been asking for Ethan. Good day."

Out of everything that the guy just told us, the news I'm struggling with most is that Dad has been asking for me. He did say that he was delusional, though, so maybe that explains it. I look over at Mom sitting in the dull grey chair against the dull blue wall of this dull fucking room. Why would they make it so depressing? It's a family room, or at least that's what it said on little white plaque on the door. I'm under no illusion of what it's used for—to deliver bad new to the patients' relatives—so why make the room so cold and miserable? The room alone makes me want to slit my goddamn wrists, and that was before the doctor came in and gave us the bad news.

"Your dad has already made all the arrangements for his death. We both have; we did it a few years back, all I need to do is contact the company that we organized it through. They'll take care of the rest."

I know she's talking to me, but it's like she's on auto-pilot: her face is completely blank, bereft of emotion and her voice is low and monotone. *I wonder if this is how I looked when he was beating me? Switched off.*

"That's one less thing for you to worry about then, I suppose. Do you want to go in and see him before me? I think I'd rather I speak to him alone if that's okay by you."

"Of course." She walks behind my chair and gives my shoulder a quick squeeze as she leaves. It's meant as a show of affection, but it's the shoulder I messed up in the accident and it sends searing hot pain down my torso. I have to clench my teeth to control my reaction. I watch her as she crosses the hall into Dad's room before the door closes and blocks my view. I pull out my phone and attach my headphones, then flick through my music until I find something to lose myself in. I'd do just about anything at the moment to escape the voices running wild in my head. They're arguing to say goodbye and be the bigger man with the ones screaming to get answers —to hell with whether or not it's an appropriate time to demand them. I'm so tired of the noise, I'm tired of the confusion, and I'm tired of life.

ele

Black Label Society is not a good band to listen to when you're half asleep. My music is on shuffle and I almost jump out of my skin when the track changes and *Stillborn* bursts out of my headphones. My heart's slamming against my chest and I'm panting in shock. I need to get a grip. I sink back into the chair and check my watch; it's been over a half an hour since mom went into his room. I'm contemplating going and knocking on the door when she walks back into the family room with two bottles of water and hands me one.

"Thanks."

"You're welcome, honey. Your dad is a little out of it; he's asking for you, but I'm not sure how long he'll be able to stay awake. He was drifting in and out as I was talking to him."

I feel the icy fingers of dread grasp at me. Suddenly the reality that I need to walk back into his room and talk to him is no longer a notion, and it scares the shit out of me. I twist the cap off of my water bottle and take a long pull as Mom watches me intently. I don't think she believes that I'll go through with at, hell; I'm not sure if I do.

"Are you sure you don't want me to come in there with you?"

I almost laugh. The concept of her wanting to help me now seems utterly futile. He can't get out of his bed and beat me, so for once, I don't need any help. Where were the offers when I was locked in the garage with him?

I can feel my temper begin to rise, and I tighten my fists a couple of times to try and shake it.

"No, I'm good," I tell her as I get up and make my way towards his room. I don't know why I'm so nervous, but I need to stand and take a few deep breaths before I finally push the door open and step inside.

"Dad?"

I walk around the bed and hesitate. I don't know if I should sit down or not. He doesn't look like himself. There's a thick layer of scruff on his face, and his hair is greasy and limp, laying flat against his forehead. He's always been clean-shaven and immaculately presented, even on days when he's not working or we've been on vacation. I don't think I've ever seen him look anything other than entirely put together. There are tubes and wires running all over his bed, and the position he's propped up in looks awkwardly unnatural. His eyes are closed and I spin on my heel and head for the door just when his gravelly voice cuts through the din of the machines breathing for him.

"Son?"

I stiffen at the use of the word; it denotes a certain amount of closeness that we don't share, and it's not what I'm accustomed to him calling me. *Prick, Ungrateful Little Shit, Waste of Space* have generally been his preferred terms of endearment toward me when there's been nobody else around to hear.

I turn slowly and meet his gaze. It's like looking at your worst nightmare and yet you're completely awake, rooted to the spot. You want to scream and run, but nothing happens. The compassion that a son should be feeling isn't there. I'm not even sure that the hate is. I'm hollow, an empty vessel that's going through the motions as we stare at each other hard.

"You've been asking for me?"

"Yes."

"Why?" I ask as I walk around to the chair at the end of his bed. I hold onto the back, rather than sit. It looks like I'm hiding behind a giant blue cushioned shield. Maybe that's how I'm using it; the subconscious does funny things, and I feel better knowing there's a barrier between us even though I know he can't move.

"Your mother and I have been talking. I guess you've been updated with my condition? Well, the truth is that my prognosis is less than rosy, and I want to get my affairs in order."

An affair, is that what I am? Just another menial inconvenience that needs to be dealt with? I'm gripping the chair as hard as I can, forcing myself not to interrupt him.

"I wanted to let you know that I don't blame you."

I'm not sure that I'm hearing him right; I watch him closely, waiting for him to carry on, but it's apparent that he's expecting my response.

"Don't blame me for what? For you being in here? Wait, no…you don't blame me for screwing up your life? Or you don't blame me for my real mother dying? Maybe you don't blame me for aggravating you and making you hit me. Come on Dad, you'll have to help me out here because there's quite a list to choose from. Which one is it that you're absolving me of?"

My knuckles have turned white from the pressure I'm applying to the back of the seat, my breathing feels labored, and I'm having a hard time maintaining control over the volume of my voice. I want to scream, toss this chair at him and let go of the rage that's simmering so close to the surface. It worries me that I may not be able to contain it much longer.

He squeezes his eyes shut and works his jaw back and forth. He doesn't have the luxury of expressing the anger and frustration I can tell he so badly wants to let out.

"I guess I deserve that. I know I've been less than a model father to you."

My sardonic laughter halts his admissions. "Model father! Damn…you must be on more drugs than I realized if you think your parenting skills can even be classified in the same realm as a model father."

It's a low blow; I don't know why I'm trying to aggravate him and pick a fight. I suppose I'm not comfortable with this situation, and when you feel out of your depths, you revert to what you know. All I've ever known with my dad is him talking down to me, shouting, complaining. I'm so used to it that it makes me uncomfortable when he's not. I don't know the last time we had a discussion that didn't end in him yelling at me about what a worthless screw up I am.

"Let me get this out, will you?" he wheezes and I can tell it's an effort for him to talk. "I know my failings. I don't need them pointed out. I wanted to tell you that I'm sorry before it's too late."

"It's already too late, Dad."

"You have every right to hate me. I've struggled for so long, watching you grow into a version of Samantha that I just couldn't deal with. Your mannerisms, appearance, everything about you reminds me of her. I know you can't help that, but you need to understand what it's like for me. Every time I look at you, I see her. Then I'm overcome with resentment, and I can't stop my anger. I'll start talking to you and my control slips and before I know it I'm not talking, I'm screaming louder and louder and I know it's wrong, but I can't stop myself.

"I thought that if I emotionally disconnected from you, it would get better. Before long I felt completely overwhelmed that I couldn't get control over the bitterness. The resentment was eating at me, and I didn't want anything to do with you. Day after day, especially when you were younger, I wanted to be left alone and for you to be quiet. That way I wouldn't have to be this monster I've become. But you always wanted my attention, my approval. You wouldn't listen. If you'd just listened, I wouldn't have had to be so strict."

I've known for a long time that he hated me, but having him confirm it to me has my whole body vibrating. I'm not sure if it's shock, anger, or hurt, even. I need to sit down. I move around the chair and drop into it like a ragdoll as my legs give way, and I clutch at chunks of my hair as I rest my elbows on my knees.

"Why did you not just give me up? Why spend your life looking after a kid you hate?"

"I don't hate you...I love you."

That has my attention; my eyes snap back to his. "Are you kidding me right now? You've just told me how much you resent me. You've basically blamed me for making you into a monster, and now you're telling me you love me. Well, fuck you!"

"Now, hold on—"

"No, you hold on! You don't get to do that. You don't get to explain the abuse away with a ten minute monologue, tag on a token 'I love you' for good measure, and think that absolves your treatment of me for my entire goddamn existence."

He struggles to respond. He's panting and I think it's because he's flustered and wants to shout back but I'm wrong. The pants turn to gasps, like he can't breathe, before his eyes begin to roll back into his head and the machines he's hooked up to begin blaring out a litany of beeps and sirens.

Teams of nurses descend on the room in a rush, lowering his headrest and frantically moving over him. I'm rooted to the spot. Should I stay or go? I'm not sure what's happening but it doesn't seem good. I can't help the morbid thoughts invading my brain *what if this is it? What if he's about to die right now?* Suddenly I'm beyond angry. How dare he say those things to me and then die. I'm not finished. I need to talk. He's had his turn and it's not fair; I want mine.

"Sorry Mr. Jamison, but I need you to leave," a nurse says, ushering me out of the room as more medical staff flood the small space around him. I don't need to be asked twice. I practically run out of the room, but instead of finding Mom I sprint down the corridors and make my way out of this torturous place. I burst through the main doors and out into the street before realizing that it's not the hospital I need to escape, or even my father—it's my own mind.

Chapter 27

Blair

THE LINE IS silent as I wait for him to speak. I can hear him breathing faintly on the other end, and my heart is in my throat as I anticipate what he's calling about. I've left Brie in my room and come into my mom's bedroom to take Ethan's call. The moment I hit the accept button and he didn't say anything I knew this needed to be a private conversation.

"I shouldn't have called you," he finally murmurs into the receiver and I can barely decipher his voice from the faint sound of the traffic behind him.

"Baby, you can always call me. What's wrong? Are you okay?"

"I suppose, yeah…no, I'm outside the hospital. Something is going on with my dad. We were talking, well, he was talking, but then he started having trouble breathing, and the staff tossed me out of the room to work on him. I didn't mean to call and upset you or anything; I just needed to hear your voice."

His voice sounds so lost and I clutch at my chest; it aches so badly for him and I wish I were there to comfort him in person.

"I'm so sorry, Ethan, that's terrible. I'm sure the doctors will be doing everything that they can. Did you get to speak with him for long?"

"Only enough time for him to tell me that he's sorry he resents me but it's kind of my fault. Oh, and he loves me!"

Disdain is dripping thickly from his voice and I actually feel my jaw gape.

"What? How is it your fault that he dislikes you? Oh my gosh, what an ass. I could kill him!"

The words escape me before I can register what I've just said. I'm a moron. Why can't I exercise my filter like an ordinary person? Who tells their boyfriend that they could kill his dad, when he's in a hospital, possibly dying!

He lets out a sarcastic huff. "I remind him of my real mom, that's why he's an asshole with me. Apparently vying for his attention when I was younger just pissed him off even more. He wanted to ignore me, and I never let him."

Wow. How do I even respond to that and attempt to lift his spirits?

"He said that?"

"More or less. He had just enough time to tell me that he still loved me though, before he lost consciousness. I know this is bad, Princess, but I'm mad as hell he said that and it might be the last thing he gets to say to me. He has no right."

Brie surges into the room wearing my 'Mathlete' t-shirt; it's knotted at the front, underneath her boobs, displaying her whole midsection.

"This is cute, can I borrow it?" She twirls and then stops in front of Mom's mirrored closet before she notices me trying to kill her with my eyes in the reflection.

"What?" she mouths innocently.

"Sorry, Ethan one second," I tell him before hugging my cell to my chest so he can't hear.

"Brie I'm on the phone!" I glare, and she stands there unmoving. "And why are you wearing my clothes?"

"It looks cute though, right? So can I borrow it?"

"Ugh…fine, yes you can borrow the shirt. Now can you please wait in my room for me? This is kind of an important call."

"Wow, someone's grouchy today. Missing your boy toy already?" she sings as she walks out of the room like she's strutting down the runway for a fashion show.

"Ethan, you still there?"

"Yeah, still here. Listen, I need to go. I'll text you later," he says sounding distracted, or maybe annoyed. Here he is spilling his heart to me and I make him hold while Brie talks about shirts.

"I'm sorry for the interruption. Brie's here and she just burst in. I've gotten rid of her now. We can carry on—"

"No, it's fine, honestly. I need to go anyway."

"Oh, um, yeah okay then. It doesn't matter what time it is; I'll be here. In case you want to call and talk some more. I love you."

I listen to him inhale loudly before he tells me he

loves me too and disconnects the call. I hate that he's hurting, and I'm not there. I sit on the end of my mom's bed and stare down at my screen, willing him to call back, but he doesn't.

I walk into my room in time to see Brie flash me her thong-clad ass as she's shimmying into an old pair of vintage Levi cut-offs. I feel like I've entered some weird alternate universe.

"What are you doing?"

"Oh, hey…I was bored. You know, you have some seriously cool pieces of clothing. These are awesome," she says, jumping up and down while hiking them over her butt and fastening them.

I laugh nervously because this is just too weird.

"Do you usually go to people's houses and try on their clothes when they're out of the room?"

"Yeah," she deadpans.

"Ha, okay, that shuts me up then. They were my mom's; they're my favorite," I tell her motioning to the shorts.

"You're mom's got awesome taste."

"Yeah, she does I suppose. She's originally from Texas. She knows how to rock a pair of cut-offs and cowboy boots." I smile then dig through the bottom of my closet before I pull out a pair of old tan boots.

"Please tell me that they're an eight and that you'll let me steal these too," she squeals snatching the boots from me.

"Actually they're an eight and a half, but sure, you can borrow them if you want."

"Really? Eek! I'm totally going to pull a Daisy Duke

on Jackson's ass. He's not gonna know what's hit him," she smirks and I laugh.

"Wait, are you wearing my clothes to try and get lucky with Jackson? Oh my gosh, ew! In fact, no. Do. Not. Answer. That!"

I shudder, and she swats at my arm.

"So, who was on the phone? You looked all moody and intense when I walked in. Wasn't interrupting anything important, was I?"

"It was Ethan, and it kind of was important, yeah."

She arches her brow no doubt waiting for me to confide in her, but it's never going to happen, and she seems to realize this as I return her wide-eyed stare.

"Ugh, You really need to learn to gossip more," she says, dropping my shorts and stepping out of them. I have no idea where to look. It seems that Brie is completely body confident and has no issue prancing around in her underwear in front of people.

I busy myself leafing through one of Em's journals sitting in the box at the foot of my bed, while Brie changes back into her own clothes. I'm conscious of her jabbering away but I've completely tuned her out as I stare down at the purple handwriting. I didn't think I'd ever see it again. The last things I read that Em had written were the letter and bucket list. I haven't looked at them since the night before the accident. I'm not sure if I'll ever be able to complete that list for her. In some ways it's the cause of so many bad things, yet I can't help but be thankful that she wrote it. Ultimately it's what led me to Ethan. Sure, I would have still been paired with him for his math tutoring, but if it wasn't for the need to cross off Emily's requests, I probably never would have gone to the party at TJ's with him, which was the starting point to the chain of events that led to us being together.

I read the first couple of lines on the page I opened to in her journal and then slam it shut quickly. I feel like I'm intruding on something that nobody was ever meant to see. They are her thoughts, dreams, worries and aspirations. She wrote them in complete abandonment, without any intention of them seeing the light of day. I place the journal back in the box, not quite ready to read it and I feel a little more downhearted as I do. I miss Em, and there's nothing I can do to take away the ache I feel when I think of her. I make a mental note to take some Gerberas to her grave and tell her how much I wish she were here right now.

"Who pissed on your cereal?" Brie asks, looking at me like maybe I've grown two heads.

"That's an awful saying. You sound like TJ, and that is definitely not a good thing."

"Low blow, Blair. I do not sound anything like TJ, but seriously, you look like you're about to cry...if you don't want to lend me the clothes, it's fine."

"No, it's not that. I couldn't care less about the clothes. I just miss Em; I went to see her parents today, and I'm in a bit of a funk, and then the phone call you walked in on with Ethan. He's having a rough time at the moment and his dad is in a really bad way, I guess I'm just letting everything get on top of me, and I feel completely useless, which I hate."

"You know what you need, right? You need a girls' night. Let's call Casey and we'll go to the movies and catch a rom-com, then go out for ice-cream, the real stuff though, none of this low fat, frozen yogurt bullshit. I'm talking Cherry Garcia, whipped cream and chocolate sauce. Whadaya say? You in?"

"You had me at Cherry Garcia…call Casey."

Chapter 28

Ethan

THE ONLY THING worse than having to spend time in a hospital is having to spend time in a hospital visiting with someone that you know can't stand you, and the feeling is mutual. The doctors have managed to stabilize Dad for the time being. His lungs had filled with fluid; apparently that's a byproduct of him having pneumonia, and no muscle control in his chest. He's still out cold, I'm not sure if he'll even come around again before visiting time is over. My mom's on edge; she doesn't know what to do or say to me and I can tell she feels horrible, it's written across her weary drawn face. The truth is, I don't know what to say to her, either. I feel so disconnected from everyone at the moment that I don't even know which way is up anymore.

The call to Blair didn't help my mood; it just made me wish I were home with her instead of here.

"Do you think he's going to die?" I say out loud, and watch as Mom continues stirring her cheap, crappy-tasting instant coffee, the type that tastes burnt no matter how you prepare it. It's the only stuff that they provide in the family room. She seems to be off in a world of her own, staring out into space.

"Hmm…what was that, honey?"

"I said do you think Dad is going to die?"

She sighs and looks down into her mug.

"I think that's a strong possibility, but I don't under-estimate your father. He's a fighter."

Yeah, and don't I know it. I lean back in the ratty old chair and rest my feet on the coffee table. I'm sick of this room already.

"The doctors don't sound too hopeful that he's going to make it through the surgery he needs. What if he does though, what do we do? Will he come home with us, or does he need to be in some sort of facility or care home? Who'll look after him?"

I know it's pretty shitty timing to ask, but it's been bothering me. It's one thing to have to exist in the same house as the asshole, but an entirely different ball game to have to become his nursemaid too.

"I haven't thought that far ahead, Ethan. I don't know what will happen, but we'll figure something out. I don't want you to be worrying about this; you'll be off to college soon anyway, so you needn't worry. I'll handle every-thing."

"I just don't see how you would cope. You need to work, and you can't be a full-time caregiver and hold down your job. You'd need to pay for someone to look after him, and that's not cheap."

She rubs her hands down her face and I know she's

217

worrying about this too.

"I know Ethan, but at the moment, we just need to fo-cus on getting him well enough so he can go through with the surgery. Once we've crossed that bridge, we can worry about what happens next."

I know she's right, but her answer unsettles me. Sit-ting back and hoping things fall in to place has never been my strong point; uncertainty unnerves me. It always has—no doubt a consequence of having an abusive father. Ever since I was a kid I've always been one for wanting to know where everyone is and what they're doing. That way I knew when to keep out of the way.

"I let you down, Ethan," Mom says, breaking through my thoughts. This whole situation—you wanting to get closure—it's all wrong. We should be sitting here worry-ing about your dad and we're not. You're worrying about him pulling through, I can tell."

"Can you blame me?" I almost spit.

"Not at all; that's the saddest part, honey. I don't blame you at all—how could I? It's my fault. I've sat by and watched for years and done nothing. Just when I thought we may finally be able to escape him, this happens and he's trapping us all over again," she chokes out and lowers herself into the chair opposite me. Her whole body is shuddering with sobs yet she's not making even the slightest sound. The thought that she's had to adapt to cry-ing silently leaves a pretty stale taste in my mouth and a heavy feeling in my chest.

"You were going to go off to school, I was going to finally leave him and now…God, Ethan, I can't leave him now. Not like this. He has nobody but us."

She looks utterly wrecked, and for the first time in so long, too long, I move over to her and place my arms around her shoulders and I let her cry. I've been consumed with feelings of animosity towards her, and even though we'll never have the kind of closeness that other families have, I do believe she's done her best. She's been trapped in a situation she didn't ask for, with an abusive husband and no parental rights to her son. I know that the only reason she's here with us now is because of her love for me.

She twists and clings to my chest as the noiseless sobs wrack though her body and her tears soak through the shoulder of my t-shirt. My head is thumping and an intense pressure is building behind my eyes. I'm not sure if it's the headache that I've been plagued with since waking up from the accident, or if this one is because I'm trying my damnedest not to cry too.

ﾟ𝓁𝓁𝑒

The nurse startles Mom as she lets the door to the family room bang shut when she enters. I sit up and lower my legs from the coffee table. Pulling out one of the buds of my headphones, I wait for her news.

"I just wanted to let you know that visiting hours will be over in ten minutes, but Mr. Jamison is awake again now if you want to say goodbye for the night."

"Thanks, we'll be right in," I answer and Mom smiles sympathetically at me.

We gather up our things, my hoody and Mom's purse, place the plastic coffee cups we've collected in the trash and follow the nurse out of the room. My mom enters first and sits in the chair at the end of his bed; I follow and stay standing behind her.

"You're still here?" he says, the surprise is evident in his week quiet tone.

"So are you?" I reply, the disappointment evident in mine. Mom shoots me a quick pleading look, as if asking me to be civil with her eyes. I take a deep breath and try muster up some strength to stand in here and not get into an argument.

"How are you feeling?" she asks Dad, and he lets out a small huff.

"Like I've been in a crash." He may have lost the use of his body, but his sarcastic nasty streak seems to have survived unscathed.

I stiffen as Mom barks out his name in warning. I can't help but feel a little pissed. I've never heard her once raise her voice to him, and I just assumed she was incapable. His eyes narrow marginally and I can tell he's thrown just as much as me by the bite to her voice.

"We were told to come and say goodnight. Visiting's over," I say and make to leave. I don't want to be in here a second longer than is necessary.

"Sit down, Ethan," Mom orders again, and now I'm really aggravated. Where the fuck was this assertiveness the rest of my life? I do as she says out of curiosity for her newfound boldness rather than anything else, and wonder what she's up to.

"Ethan will be leaving to go back home in the morning," she announces to my dad, and it's the first I've heard of it too. "He has lots to catch up on before graduation and he has hospital appointments he shouldn't miss."

"What hospital appointments?" Dad asks, his eyes skimming me for signs of injury.

"I have physiotherapy for my wrist, and I need to see the neuropsychologist about my memory," I offer, shortly.

"What's wrong with your memory?"

"I told you this already, Frank. He was in a coma after the accident. He hurt his head...remember?"

I'm not sure if it's annoyance that Mom's answered his question, or if its concern I detect in his expression.

"Are you okay?" he asks and I let out a disbelieving laugh.

"What does it matter to you? You've never once given me a second thought when you've beat me unconscious; why's this any different? You hate me."

"Mom spins again, regarding me with a horrified look and I shrug. "What, it's the truth!" I state indignantly.

"Stop saying that. I do not hate you!" Dad raises his voice shakily, and we both turn to look at him.

"I've never hated you," he says evenly. "I told you earlier, I can't control my anger with you. You ignite memories and feelings that I spend every damn day trying to bury, and it's relentless. I know what I put you through isn't right. I just can't help it and I...I can't control it. I can't stop myself. I'm sorry, Ethan. God, you'll never understand how sorry I truly am."

I squeeze my eyes shut tight and shake my head; I don't want to hear that he's sorry, sorry doesn't cut it.

"I should never have let it get to this either. I should have protected you and I didn't." I open my eyes and even though she's speaking to me, she's staring at Dad.

"I shouldn't have put him or you in a situation that

needed protecting from me," he tells her.

"Two minutes please, and then I'll have to ask you to leave," the nurse from earlier says as she pops her head around the door smiling kindly. She takes in the look of anger on my face and the tears staining my mom's and pauses for a second before thinking better of it and her head disappears out of the room again.

"This is all bullshit. I'm not standing in here and having some pity party where you both say sorry for failing me!" I yell. "I'm not forgiving you, if that's what you're asking for!" I shout at my dad. "I didn't ask for any of this. I can't help reminding you of someone I never even got to meet. It's not my fault if I look or act like her. You've punished me my whole fucking life for something that I have no way of controlling, All I ever wanted when I was younger was for you to be proud of me. I never stood a chance though, did I? You were too busy trying to pretend I didn't exist until I annoyed you enough to beat me and make yourself feel better."

My voice cracks and I feel hot tears spill across my cheeks. I hate it. I hate that he's seeing me cry. I always promised myself that I wouldn't let him see me cry.

I want to rip this whole damn room apart and smash something. I want someone else to hurt as much as I am right now.

I want Blair.

Mom's standing now, too. She attempts to hug me but I shrug away from her.

"You know why I'm here? I didn't even want to come," I say spitefully. "I'm here because she," I point at Mom, "and my girlfriend persuaded me that I needed to gain some closure in case you died," I bellow at my dad. "Well here it is—here's my parting speech. Honestly, I hope it's the last thing I ever have to say to you: NO, I DO NOT FORGIVE YOU!

"I never will. You treated me like your worst enemy and I was a kid, just a kid. I always thought it was my fault, and you let me. The only reason you're saying sorry now is because you're scared that you're going to die and want to make peace. Well, screw you! I hope you go to hell where you belong," I sob, then turn and head to the door. I turn around to see that his eyes are red and welled up.

Good.

"I'll see you back at the hotel," I manage to say to Mom, and she nods, looking downright shattered as I walk out of the room. I brace myself on the wall and try to catch my breath. I'm crying and can't seem to get enough oxygen. I think maybe I'm having a panic attack. I crouch down and place my head between my knees and try to calm down but it's not working.

"Ethan!" Dad shouts as the door falls closed slowly. There's alarm in his voice.

"Are you okay, there?" a male doctor in a pair of blue scrubs asks, kneeling next to me. I look at him in fear. I can only see his furrowed brow and a pair of concerned brown eyes until he pulls his mask from his mouth. I can't speak through the gasping and my vision begins to swim, causing his features to blur together into one dark tan mass.

The pressure behind my eyes feels like it's reached breaking point, and my head is about to explode. I fall onto my ass and my chest begins to burn. I wonder if I'm about pass out, or maybe suffocate and die right here. I stop trying to fight for more air as I realize death would be welcomed. The blue figure next to me is laying me down onto the floor and shouting something but I can't tell what through the ringing in my ears. My head hurts too much and I close my eyes and wish for everything to just stop.

Please stop.

I'm too tired. I don't want to live like this anymore. Suddenly Blair is standing above me, smiling. She looks so beautiful as she reaches down and touches my face and then everything is still.

The noise disappears, my chest stops burning and the pressure dissipates... and then so does she.

Chapter 29

Blair

THE BUZZ IN Joe's is lightening my mood, it always does. Dad used to bring Em and me here sometimes after school if he was home from the office early enough. He'd show up outside school and announce that it was an ice cream kind of day, then we'd jump in the car and head to Joe's. Our orders were always the same. Dad would get a ridiculously large banana split with extra whip, even though he didn't particularly like cream, and then when it came, complain that there was too much and give it to me. He knew I loved it. Em would order a chocolate sundae every time without fail, and I would order a strawberry sundae with extra chocolate sauce and cherries.

"Seriously guys, if I eat any more I think I'm going to be sick," Casey says, pushing her dish aside. She wriggles in her seat and pulls at her waistband, stretching it out and making a show of trying to create more room.

"You cannot be passing up perfectly good ice

cream?" Brie says skeptically, before leaning over and scooping the remainder into her bowl. I have no idea how someone so thin can eat the way that she does and not gain weight. She's tiny but she eats like a dude.

Casey pulls up her hot pink tank and rubs at her washboard stomach.

"Ugh…sorry guys but it's gotta happen," she says popping the button on her skinny jeans and letting out an embarrassingly loud groan.

"Oh my god, that feels so good."

I laugh as Brie rolls her eyes and says, "Casey, you sound like you're about to have an orgasm."

My eyes widen at Brie's comment. This place is heaving with families and little kids.

"Oh…oh…oh, yeah. That's it…mmmmm," Casey moans and I sink low into my seat and grab a menu to shield my face.

Brie busts out laughing and for the life of me I can't understand how they are both not mortified. I peek over the menu to see two guys staring over with huge grins plastered on their faces, and a woman with two little boys next to them shooting us daggers.

"What the hell was that?" I exclaim in a whisper-shout. "Everyone's staring."

"Relax," they both answer at the same time.

"Jinx! Jinks again!" they shout and then proceed to punch each other in the arm.

"Ouch, that's going to bruise!" Casey whines and Brie smirks.

"Have you never seen *When Harry Met Sally*?" Brie asks through a mouthful of whipped cream and I wince back into my seat.

"Yeah, I have. I just wasn't expecting a reenactment in front of a bunch of kids!"

"Chill, Blair…we're only messing around. It's not like we're drunk and cussing up a storm."

I groan but concede the fact and sit up taller in the booth.

Brie purposely drips cream on her chest and then scoops it up slowly and sucks it off her finger, the two dudes mesmerized at her display. She flashes them a devilish smile and I elbow her in the side.

"What the hell, I thought you and Jackson were dating?"

"We are!" she laughs. "Those guys have been looking over at us since we came in so I thought I might as well give them something worth staring at."

Casey shakes her head, smiling at her as I sit here utterly perplexed.

"You'll get a reputation acting like that," I say. "I bet that's something Della would do!"

"Ohhh, no you did not!" Casey says finger snapping.

I'm startled out of my stupor by the sound of my cell and I have to slide out of the booth to retrieve it from my back pocket. My smile slips as the screen flashes 'Moira' and I can't help but feel instantly disappointed. I've been waiting for Ethan to call for hours now.

"Hi Moira, how are you?" I turn from the girls and head to the doorway, away from all the hustle and bustle of the other diners so I can hear better. The line is completely silent and I pull the phone from my ear and look down at the screen to make sure that I hit accept, or that I haven't accidently cut her off. It's lit up like the call is still active. "Hello? Moira, are you there?"

I hear a sniffle and then her voice, quietly on the other end of the line.

"Yes, Blair I'm here, I...I..."

She's crying and my stomach churns. This can't be good.

"Are you okay? Has something happened to Frank?"

"No honey, um...it's Ethan."

I freeze mid-step and my stomach lurches, threatening to expel the truckload of ice cream I just consumed.

"What do you mean it's Ethan? What's wrong? What's happened?"

I know before she answers that whatever she needs to say is bad, and I brace myself for it. I'm waiting for, *'He's left and won't speak to Frank,'* or *'We've had an argument'* to come, but it doesn't.

"Sweetheart, he collapsed in the hospital and...and ..." she's sobbing so hard that I can't make out what she's trying to tell me.

"Moira, I can't hear you!" I shout into the cell. I'm not sure why I'm the one shouting, she seems to be able to hear me just fine but the anxiety and fear she's causing has me jittery.

She proceeds to tell me something about a subdural hematoma and I fall to the ground. An old man with his grandchildren rushes to help me up and I feel overwhelmingly dizzy.

"Are you alright there, miss?" the old man asks as I stare at him blankly, not quite understanding what's going on.

"She dropped her phone, Grandpa," a little girl with chocolate sauce smeared all over her face says pointing to my cell, still licking her cone.

The gentleman picks it up and passes it back to me as Casey and Brie rush over and assure him they'll take over. I grab my cell and look back and forth from them. Casey's hunched over me, her long raven hair falling in my face. She pulls it to one side and holds it back as I'm frozen, trying to process what's going on, wondering if this is all some twisted sick dream. The buildup of tears and hammering in my chest let me know that it's not.

Chapter 30

Blair

I CAN HEAR soft piano music filtering through the muggy afternoon air as I cross the threshold, making my way down the cold stone aisle towards the altar. I can feel people staring, their gazes penetrating my skin as if each one physically presses upon me with the intensity of a searing hot branding iron. I'm all too conscious of the hushed whispers floating around in the desolate space. I'm shivering as I make my way to the front; I can't get a hold on my nerves. Voices that I don't recognize are uttering, "Is that the girlfriend? She was in the accident too, wasn't she?" They infiltrate my senses. Are these people really so ignorant that they have all forgotten this place is designed to carry noise? Each comment I catch as I near my destination feels more scathing than the last. I focus my attention on the vast grandeur of the stained-glass window at the front of the church and watch as the sun's midday rays pass through the colored panes, casting a rainbow that cascades down over the congregation of mourners. The bright hues are a stark disparity against the sea of black suits and white-collared shirts. There doesn't seem to be a single fleck of color on anyone's clothing, except the gold and red of the police decorations pinned proudly to the uniformed officers sporting them. Their brightness a welcomed break in the monotonous army of glum clones.

My fingers are closed tightly around the stem of a single white rose. I didn't know if I should bring flowers or not, but now I wish I hadn't. I need to walk over to his coffin to lay it down; I hadn't thought of that. Bile rises in my throat, and the tears that have formed are threatening to fall. I'm holding my breath, eyes wide, willing them to dissipate as I return my focus once more to the window instead of the casket. It's too soon to be doing this again. The painful memory of Emily's funeral, still raw and exposed, sits unwelcomingly at the forefront of my mind. It's playing on an agonizing loop, taunting me, reminding me. The aesthetics couldn't be more different from hers, though; Emily's funeral service was akin to walking into a child's birthday party. Balloons adorned the ends of each pew in varying shades of shiny pink and purple latex. Cheerful, bright gerberas had been placed on every available surface, and there wasn't a single solitary piece of black clothing to be found. We had been given explicitly strict instructions to wear 'happy clothes' or she would 'haunt our asses for all eternity.' Em's words, not mine. There was to be no gloomy piano music, either; no nineties power-ballads of heartache and pain. Instead, the church was filled with dubiously dulcet tones from One Direction's *Story of My Life*. I'd practically scoffed when Em announced to me that she'd found the perfect funeral song. She proceeded to tell me that she'd narrowed it down to 1D or Bon Jovi's *Sleep When I'm Dead*. In any other circumstance, I'd have voted Bon Jovi all the way, but I had to concede on this one. I almost smile at the memory before realizing where I am and what I'm doing.

I slow my pace down, not wanting to reach my destination, but there's no avoiding it. In the next three steps I've reached the coffin. I can't prolong the inevitable any longer; I look down at the long mahogany box laid before me topped with what must be hundreds of roses. My whole body trembles as I reach out to place my flower amongst the other tributes. I catch my reflection against the highly polished surface of the wood and begin to feel dizzy. I blink attempting to refocus my vision as my fingers loosen their grip on the rose. My hand brushes against the cold hardwood and I pause briefly, wondering if it's time to wake up yet. Wishing for a different reality to the one I'm in at the moment. I hear Ethan's mom softly call out my name, but I can't move. I'm frozen in place by…I don't even know what, fear? Memories?

"Blair, honey…come sit by me." It's an order rather than request; suddenly she's by my side and ushering me to take a seat. I let her lead the way; it's just her sitting upfront.

"My mom couldn't find a parking spot; she'll be here any minute, is it okay for her to sit here too?"

"Of course, it is," she says and smiles weakly. "You're family."

I take in her appearance: her eyes are puffy and tired, and she looks completely worn out and defeated- her cheeks look hollow, her hair is sitting limply on her shoulders and her lips are cracked and set into a thin line, She's a shadow of the woman Ethan first introduced me to months ago. The piano music stops and a minister approaches the lectern. I look wide-eyed at Moira and then glance at the empty seat where my mom should be right now. I need her here; I can't do this without her. I can't bear to sit through another funeral. Moira senses my anxiety and runs her hand down over my hair; she squeezes my shoulders and then pulls me into her side like my mom would do. The minister starts to speak, but I don't hear any words through the sound of the blood rushing in my ears. I can't do this. I'm not ready. I blink and let my first tear fall, no doubt carving the way for more to follow. I had agreed to come for Moira. I felt bad that she would have to face this alone. I look blankly towards the front but I can't see anything past my pain.

I'm drawn out of my trance by the shuffling beside me. I let my eyelids drop closed as I say a silent prayer thanking God for answering my pleas and not making me endure this alone. The gentle feel of fingers lacing through my own calm my racing pulse and muffle the drumming of my heart against my chest, dulling it just enough for the discomfort to begin to subside. I squeeze my hand slightly as an indication of my gratitude. My anxiety wanes enough to allow my other senses to take purchase on my surroundings. For the first time I become conscious of the sound of the minister's voice leading the service and I straighten my back and sit taller in my seat, deciding that I'm not going to be defeated by today. I allow myself the belief that I'm stronger than I give myself credit for.

The minister begins a reading that elicits an audible sigh from my lips, and it escapes into the air in a short sharp burst. The reading is the same one I gave at my father's funeral. There's no way that Moira could have known that this one passage can undoubtedly break my all-too weak resolve, the one I'd found only seconds ago. I couldn't stop the tears from falling now, even if I wanted to, as I listen to the verse being spoken, my mind tracing each one of W. H. Auden's words.

Stop all the clocks, cut off the telephone
Prevent the dog from barking with a juicy bone
Silence the pianos and with muffled drum
Bring out the coffin, let the mourners come.
Let airplanes circle moaning overhead
Scribbling on the sky the message He Is Dead,
Put crepe bows round the white necks of the public doves;
Let the traffic policemen wear black cotton gloves.
He was my North, my South, my East and West,
My working week and my Sunday rest.
My noon, my midnight, my talk, my song;
I thought that love would last forever; I was wrong.
The stars are not wanted now, put out every one;
Pack up the moon and dismantle the sun.
Pour away the ocean and sweep up the wood,
For nothing now can ever come to any good.

I know the verse as if I'd penned it myself. I was the one to pick it for my father. I'd heard it spoken in a film that Em once made me watch. I remember thinking how powerful it was, and it never really left me. When my dad died, Mom was a mess. She handled everything with grace and left nothing undone, but when it came to choosing the readings; it was as if the weight of what had happened descended on her all at one. She was sitting at the kitchen table, going through the order of service and then suddenly she was smashing glasses and screaming *'why'*. We sat for hours amongst the broken pieces just holding one another. When she finally stopped sobbing I told her that I would organize the reading. She looked so relieved that I didn't dare tell her I was terrified. Instead, I spent hours Googling passages that were deemed suitable for funerals, and then I came across Auden's piece and recognized it immediately. I read it over and over for the next two days until I could practically recite it in my sleep.

I look at our hands intertwined in my lap, and my tears drip onto our skin. Ethan gives me a small smile, and I look across him to my mom. Her own tears are sliding in a steady stream down her face, and I know hearing this will be pulling back all the memories I have just experienced for her too.

I watch as he takes a hold of her hand like he has mine before turning to press a soft kiss to my temple. I'm not sure what my mom said to him outside but she somehow managed to change his mind to come inside. I'm more thankful to her than I'll ever be able to express, for my sake and his.

I glance at Ethan's face to see how he's doing and my eyes are instantly drawn to the side of his head where the stitches are still all visible from his surgery.

When Mom and I flew out to the hospital after Moira's phone call, she, along with the help of one of the doctors, explained to us what had happened. Ethan had suffered from a chronic subdural hematoma. The doctor said that it was normal after experiencing a head injury, as Ethan had in the crash, to have headaches. The symptoms of a chronic subdural hematoma don't usually appear until a few weeks after the initial head injury, and then progress gradually. We all knew that Ethan was suffering from headaches, but thought it was normal. He'd been feeling dizzy more and more, and didn't have an appetite, but with everything going on it was overlooked as stress. I certainly hadn't picked up on it, and I'm the one person that spent the most time with him. Sitting in that hospital realizing that almost ate me alive with guilt. The doctors—and even moreso, Moira—had assured me that a chronic subdural hematoma can be difficult to detect and can go unrecognized for some time. I was so mad that no one had warned me to look out for signs that I shouted at the doctor before breaking down in floods of tears. It was only luck that he happened to be in the hospital when he collapsed, and he had access to treatment so quickly.

He catches me staring and squeezes my hand again. The side of his head had to be shaved, so now he's sporting a cut that's super short at the back and sides, and then messy and longer on top. Only Ethan could make post-op hair look sexy.

The minister finishes his reading and invites one of Frank's superiors up to speak a few words. Ethan stiffens as the gentleman in uniform talks of what a well-respected police offer, member of the community, husband and father Frank was. I'm half-expecting that he may stand and leave, but he doesn't. Instead he sits and listens, and I can tell that he's trying hard.

ele

"I'm going for a drive with Blair," he announces to his mom, after the millionth person comes to speak to him at the wake, telling him how sadly missed his father will be and what a great guy he was.

"Okay, sweetheart," she replies and my mom, who's sipping a cup of tea next to her, smiles her approval. He takes my hand and wastes no time leading me out towards my car in a hurry. We step out onto the lawn, and he pauses and takes a long deep breath.

"You okay?" I ask.

"I am now. I'm so glad to be out of that damn house! I don't think I could have stood there a second longer and listened to anyone else tell me what a great guy he was."

I don't blame his eagerness to get out of the house, and in truth, it was getting to me too. It's hard to stand back and listen to people speak so highly of someone that you know is undeserving of their ill-placed praise.

"Jackson and the guys are still in there; do you want me to go and tell them we're leaving?"

"Don't worry about it, I'll text them. I just want to get out of here now. Do you mind driving?" he asks, and I smirk.

"You're going to let me drive your car?" I ask hopefully, knowing full well he doesn't entirely trust me in his Camaro because I suck at driving stick.

"Not a chance, Princess, that's why we're standing at

yours."

"Huh, fine." I sniff and then stick my tongue out.

"You're acting like a child, Ms. Thomas," he states mockingly.

"Whatever—you know you love it." I smile and open the passenger door for him.

I'm grabbed by the waist as he pulls me tightly into him, slamming his lips against mine and pinning me against the side of the car.

"Yeah, I do," he murmurs through our kiss and I feel myself melt into him. He taps my butt and instructs me to drive him to the beach, so that's what I do.

elle

We sit on the cooling gold sand for a long time, staring out at the ocean before he decides to finally speak. "I talked with my doctor yesterday," he informs me, and I pause. He'd never mentioned that he had an appointment. "I told her how I was feeling, about some of the morbid thoughts I had. I told her about the abuse with Dad and she's referred me to a psychotherapist."

I whip my head around so fast in surprise that I unbalance myself and have to throw my arms out, to keep from toppling over. He smiles down at me and nudges his arm against my shoulder.

"Relax, that doesn't mean I'm a psycho," he says widening his eyes in a demented fashion and I laugh.

"I know it doesn't!"

"She thinks that I'll benefit by learning about my feelings and thoughts towards my dad. I told her that when he'd died of the pneumonia, the night after I'd collapsed. I wasn't upset, but relieved and she said that psychotherapy would help me learn how to deal with feelings like that, to take control of my life and respond to 'challenging situations' as she called them. Honestly I had to kind of smile. Who talks like that about death? Anyway...yeah, apparently it should help to teach me healthy coping skills, and how to process all the negative thoughts I have in association with him."

"Ethan, that's amazing," I tell him and watch the apprehension drain from his face.

"Yeah, you think so? You're not worried that your boyfriend needs therapy?"

I move and straddle his lap and cradle his face with my hands.

"I am so proud of you; you have no idea. The fact that you've decided to get help with this astounds me. Your strength astounds me. So, no baby, I'm not in any way, shape, or form worried about my boyfriend being in therapy." I kiss his forehead and then lean back and watch his dimples pop as he gives me a genuine, beautiful smile. "You're kind of amazing," I tell him.

"Yeah, most chicks think that."

I narrow my gaze and he winks.

"Okay, I've changed my mind; you're a jackass!"

"Maybe, but I'm all yours," he tells me, before flipping me over and pushing me down into the sand as he kisses me breathless.

"I'm yours, too," I murmur against the softness of his lips.

"Promise?"

"Promise."

Epilogue

Blair

"HELLO AND WELCOME to the commencement ceremony for West Point's graduating class of 2014."

I pause and look out over the sea of purple caps. My palms are sweating and I realize that although I've been leading up to this point for my whole high school career, being up here now is slightly terrifying. Especially since the speech I've had ready for the best part of ten months is sitting in the trash can in my bedroom, and the one I'm looking at now was written last night.

"Can you believe that we actually made it? Or most of us, at least. Before I get started I'd just like to ask the guys who are busy posting random graduation selfies to kindly let me steal your attention and please listen to this speech. It won't take long. I hopefully have some insightful words of wisdom to impart. Although, don't feel like you have to switch off your cells—I'm more than happy for you to upload this speech onto YouTube. I'm sure anyone who knows me will confirm that it's highly plausible I'll mess up and say something inappropriate, or fall getting down from this podium, and you wouldn't want to miss it. Be sure to hashtag my name. It's Blair without an E." I let out a nervous laugh as the auditorium is deathly silent. I'm half-expecting a tumbleweed to materialize and blow across the stage.

"Anyway, moving on. I want to take a second and ask you all to think of how much it's taken for you to even be here right now. There are a few people I know who would have loved to be sitting and experiencing this day with the rest of us. My best friend Emily Wilson, you've no doubt heard of her, wanted to make it to this day badly. It was her goal and one that she fought hard to achieve. But fate had a different plan.

I want to share something that Em once wrote in her journal, and I think it's pretty apt for today.

I once heard someone say that life begins at the end of your comfort zone, but what they didn't take into account was people like me. I'm completely out of my comfort zone. I take seven different types of medication every single day, I'm slowly killing my body, poisoning it with chemicals in a bid to save it. I'm eating myself from the inside out, so I think that qualifies as being out of my comfort zone. But life isn't guaranteed to begin just beyond this…Life is now, right this second while I'm sitting here breathing, my lungs inflating and my heart beating—this is my life.

People shouldn't constantly strive to do things that scare them in a bid to live, otherwise their lives will be filled with fear. Similarly, they shouldn't sit around wait-ing for something epic that sparks their realization that their life has just begun.

Life is what happens while you're waiting for it to happen. It's not always extraordinary. Most people won't get to realize all of their hopes and dreams, but they'll be living out new ones they never knew they wanted. Spend-ing time worrying about the future, about getting into col-lege and carving out a meaningful life won't empty tomor-row of its plights, it will simply drain today of its vitality.

I haven't always believed in destiny, but today I was told mine: my cancer has won and science can do no more. My destiny has been pre-written, and no matter what I do now, I can't re-write it. But I can live until my heart stops beating. I WILL live. I'm going to start each day smiling and extract every molecule of happiness it has to offer, because my life may be short, but I'm determined to make it full.

I pause to collect my thoughts and steady my breath-ing; my eyes are welled and I need a second for the mois-ture to disappear and stop blurring my vision. I look out to the crowd and spot my mom sitting between Emily's par-ents and Moira.

I hadn't known that Pam and Bill would be here to-day. When I saw them before I had to take my place in the auditorium, they told me that they wouldn't have missed my graduation for the world, and they're only sorry that they didn't get to witness Em's too. I was so choked that I couldn't warn them that I would be reading from her diary. I can see Bill rubbing Pam's back as she blots furiously at her face with a hanky, but they are both beaming proudly. My anxiety begins to wane and I carry on.

"Emily's words made me think, and I hope that they strike a chord with you too. So I'm not going to tell you to strive to achieve greatness; instead, I'm going to say stop doing things that you don't want to do. If you don't want to study pre-med, but you're planning on it anyway, because your father, and your grandfather and his father all did...just stop. Do the things that YOU want to do, because this isn't a dress rehearsal, this is the main event.

Say what you really mean, follow your intuition and let yourself be inspired, because someday you may become someone else's inspiration. Be good to yourself and don't be afraid to say no. Don't be afraid to say yes! Try not to look back, because that's not the direction you're travelling, and don't worry, because it's okay to not have a plan. Not everyone knows at eighteen what they want to do, and how it is that they are going to get there. Sometimes we need to just breathe, let everything go and see what happens.

Today is our last day as high school students, and if anything, it has made me realize that life is short. So laugh when you can, apologize when you should, and make every day count. No doubt some of you will be feeling ecstatic that school is now over. Some melancholy, some bored, and I'm sure although many won't admit it, there's even a few of us feeling a little heartbroken. Enjoy these feelings—they're how you know you're alive.

Congratulations, Class of 2014!"

Silence descends and although I wasn't expecting a fanfare, I didn't count on nothing at all. I look out to the crowd and then I spot him. He's wearing the biggest grin I've ever seen grace his handsome face.

Ethan stands and slowly begins to clap, then Brie appears and follows suit, then Case, Jackson and TJ, before the whole senior class takes to the floor and begins applauding. I smile at the sight I'm witnessing and taste a rogue tear as it slides down my cheek and wets the corner of my mouth.

For the first time since Emily died, I'm excited for the future.

The End

Thank YOU

AS WITH *Promises Hurt*, I am beginning my acknowledgements with another apology. To my amazing husband and children: I'm sorry I broke my promises…You have had to endure the microwave meals, creased clothes and a messy house again! I'm lucky that you are all so understanding and patient. I love you. You are my world.

Author Kathryn Andrews, my book bestie. You've spent countless hours helping me hash out this book and your support astounds me. I always look forward to our daily chats and voice tags. Thank goodness for Instant Messenger! You've provided so much encouragement, and you are truly a dear friend. I can't wait for our next meet up; I'll bring the pink champagne.

To all the wonderful bloggers that have loved *Promises Hurt* and supported me with *Forgotten Promises*, you guys rock! I need to single out Perusing Princess Blog. Elizabeth, Kelly and Emma; you have gone above and beyond anything I could have ever dreamed of. You have spent so much time and effort promoting me, organizing my blog tours, and I want you to know that I think you girls are just the best! To all the other super star Bloggers that have posted teasers and reviews, Thank you from the bottom of my heart. I owe you all so much. Please know that every single one of you is appreciated. Your help has been invaluable. I'll be indebted to you forever.

My BETA girls! Jaime, Silvia, Malinda, Dana, Susan, Ali and Pauline. I sent you out my manuscript knowing your feelings about the ending of book one, and I was so nervous for your comments. I had no expectations to manage with that book, but I knew you all had strong feelings on what you wanted from this one and WOW didn't expect the reactions I received. Ali —your voice message left me speechless and in happy tears! I had hoped that you would like the direction that this book takes; I never expected you to all come back and tell me that you loved it. I'm blessed to have you in my corner.

To my best friend and sister-in-law, Lucy. You are a lifesaver! Thank you so much for taking the time to cast your beady teacher eye over my manuscript, and proof it for me. You are like superwoman, helping me whilst taking care of my brand new beautiful baby niece and her gorgeous sister. Love you.

The Pimpers… Author Anne Mercier, Trish, Dana, Sanne, Alexis, Susan, Heather, Pauline, Lynn and Ali. Thank you for telling everyone about my books. You girls never fail to make me smile.

The wonderfully talented *Melissa Gill* of MGBOOK-COVERS & DESIGNS. You knocked it out of the park AGAIN!

Marie Piquette The best editor a girl could have. You are a dream to work with. I can't commend you highly enough!

Julie (JT Formatting) my brilliant formatter, you are the most helpful person ever. Thank you for squeezing me in...again! YOU ARE AWESOME.

Finally, a huge thank you to you the reader; it is still blowing my mind that you're reading my second novel after loving the first. I could never have imagined your reactions. I am so humbled.

FOR INFORMATION ABOUT ELLE BROOKS AND
HER BOOKS, VISIT:

Her Website: http://ellebrooksauthor.com

Twitter: https://twitter.com/@ellebrooksautho

E-mail: ellebrooksauthor@gmail.com

Facebook: https://facebook.com/elle.brooks.author

Goodreads: https://Goodreads.com/Elle_Brooks

THE PROMISES SERIES:

Book #1 *Promises Hurt*
Book #2 *Forgotten Promises*
Book #3 Will be coming early 2015

www.ingramcontent.com/pod-product-compliance
Lightning Source LLC
Chambersburg PA
CBHW051425170626
46809CB00006B/2332